Okinawa: Two Postwar Novellas

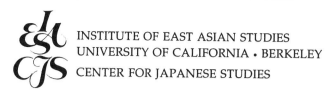

INSTITUTE OF EAST ASIAN STUDIES
UNIVERSITY OF CALIFORNIA • BERKELEY
CENTER FOR JAPANESE STUDIES

Okinawa: Two Postwar Novellas

by Ōshiro Tatsuhiro and Higashi Mineo

Translated with an introduction and afterword by
STEVE RABSON

A publication of the Institute of East Asian Studies, University of California, Berkeley. Although the Institute is responsible for the selection and acceptance of manuscripts in this series, responsibility for the opinions expressed and for the accuracy of statements rests with their authors.

The Japan Research Monograph series is one of several publications series sponsored by the Institute of East Asian Studies in conjunction with its constituent units. The others include the China Research Monograph series, the Korea Research Monograph series, the Indochina Research Monograph series, and the Research Papers and Policy Studies series. Recent titles are listed at the back of the book.

Send correspondence to

Joanne Sandstrom, Managing Editor
Institute of East Asian Studies
2223 Fulton St., 6th Fl.
Berkeley, California 94720-2318
E-mail: easia@uclink.berkeley.edu

Cocktail Party (Ōshiro Tatsuhiro's *Kakuteru pātī*) translated with author's permission.
Child of Okinawa (Higashi Mineo's *Okinawa no shōnen*) translated with author's permission.

For Yoko and Kenji

Contents

Preface

Half a century after the clash of Japanese and American forces devastated Okinawa in the spring of 1945, wide areas of Japan's southernmost prefecture remain an armed bastion. U.S. military rule in Okinawa, which lasted twenty years longer than the occupation of mainland Japan, finally ended in 1972 when this largest island in the Ryūkyū chain reverted to Japanese sovereignty. But airfields, artillery ranges, ammunition depots, infantry training grounds, and other installations still occupy 85 square miles on this island 67 miles long and an average 6¾ miles wide. Stationed here are some 30,000 American and 6,000 Japanese military personnel who live in varying degrees of isolation from Okinawa's one million residents.

On an island of such spectacular natural beauty, the effects of this massive presence have startled many first-time visitors. The landscape varies from lively business centers of stores and office buildings in the prefectural capital of Naha to quiet farming and fishing villages nestled among steep, forested hills in the countryside. Semitropical in climate, Okinawa is famous for miles of serene beaches where undersea coral formations color the warm waters in deep blues and greens. Low clouds of puffy mists hover over the ocean as in a Japanese ink-brush painting. But emerald seas and soft clouds become an incongruous backdrop for long convoys of olive-drab trucks moving through villages along the coast. Lines of fighter planes thunder into the sky from an air force base that covers much of the island's central plain. In rice fields just beyond its runways, green shoots rustle and irrigation pools shudder as passing schoolchildren press their palms over their ears. To the north, rolling sugarcane fields are barely separated by narrow dirt roads from the close-cropped lawns and flat barracks of infantry training bases. While farmers in straw sun hats tend their crops, squads of marines in full battle gear march by on the roads in loose formation toward the sounds of small arms and mortar fire coming from nearby practice ranges. To the west, the peaks of dark green hills show bald patches dotted with blinking aerials, revolving radar dishes, and high circular fences enclosing towers of antennae. And in certain towns near the larger bases, blocks of bookshops, pharmacies, and grocery stores face streets lined with bars bearing English names in neon: "Lone Star," "Nashville," and "Funky Broadway."

People in Okinawa Prefecture continue to protest the shortages of land, daily disruptions, and not infrequent dangers associated with this vast military presence that was mostly unaffected by U.S. force reductions elsewhere since the late 1980s. In mainland Japan the considerable attention of reporters and politicians shifted away from Okinawa for a time after its reversion to Japanese sovereignty and the end of U.S. involvement in Vietnam, staged in large part from bases on the island. But in recent years the effect of bases in Okinawa and other prefectures on the lives of local residents is provoking renewed concern throughout Japan.

In contrast, aside from anniversaries of the 1945 battle, Americans hear about Okinawa nowadays, if at all, only at such times as when a helicopter crash killed seventeen U.S. servicemen in 1985 or when a force of U.S. Marines was deployed from there to the Persian Gulf in 1990. The case in which two marines and one sailor were convicted in the 1995 kidnap and rape of a 12-year-old elementary school girl sparked mass demonstrations against the U.S. military presence and was widely covered in the American press. Still, few people in other countries know much about conditions in Okinawa today or the occupation that lasted an extra twenty years because U.S. policymakers considered unilateral control of the island essential to the U.S. military mission in Asia.

In a century when people in many places have lived under military occupation or martial law, U.S. rule in Okinawa seems relatively benevolent by comparison. Aside from the enforced confinement of civilians to refugee camps after the battle in 1945, there were no massive detentions. Some opposition leaders were arrested later for political activities, but people were not subjected to physical torture, firing squads, or other horrors often associated with military regimes. Although the appropriation of land for bases displaced thousands of people, the U.S. government eventually adopted a policy of rental payments and contributed annual subsidies to the troubled Okinawan economy during the occupation. And finally, after years of bilateral meetings in Tokyo and Washington, the United States agreed to reversion in 1969 when growing discontent on the island over a variety of issues threatened the utility of U.S. bases. Although this was achieved under some duress, Okinawa has now been restored to Japanese sovereignty while Russia refuses to negotiate the status of Japan's northern islands occupied by Soviet forces at the end of World War II.

Nevertheless, twenty-seven years of U.S. military rule in Okinawa profoundly affected the material, social, and psychological life of local residents. Besides seizing large tracts of cultivated farmland, the U.S. command controlled sources of power and water, managed transportation, regulated travel to and from the mainland, and imposed restrictions in spheres ranging from labor organization and capital investment to children's education and display of the Japanese flag. The spin-off economic benefits that accrued early from U.S. government projects and purchases were soon heavily outweighed by the stifling effects of a military-service economy. And although elections of local officials and a representative assembly were gradually permitted, the American generals commanding the occupation maintained and, on occasion, used their powers to revoke the assembly's legislation, overrule local government policies, and remove elected officials from office. Furthermore, the U.S. military's retention of ultimate civil and criminal jurisdiction over everyone on the island—soldiers and civilians alike—resulted in horrendous miscarriages of justice involving crimes committed by U.S. military personnel against Okinawa residents.

At a time of heightened controversy among Japanese and American scholars looking back on the occupation of Japan, this book grew out of a conviction that works of literature often provide the best means for understanding how people live in unusual circumstances. To be sure, the press in Japan produced countless words and pictures about "the Okinawa issue" during the years it was a cause célèbre. Articles, films, and television reports appeared often. And although many tended toward the superficial or sensational, they helped to stimulate awareness on the mainland of what people in Okinawa went through during and after the war, a subject barely mentioned in public school textbooks. The campaign for reversion also inspired political and philosophical writings across a wide spectrum of opinion. Some authors called for the restoration of national territory; others focused on American rule in Okinawa to protest U.S. military policies and the Japanese government's cooperation in them. The issue also stimulated interest throughout Japan in the island's history and culture to an extent that, ironically, might not have developed had Okinawa been spared invasion during the war and remained a Japanese prefecture afterward. Scholars from Okinawa and the mainland published numerous studies of traditional poetry, dance, music, religious practices, and regional dialects all of which carry certain distinctions from those in other parts of Japan. Still, by far the most sensitive and enduring portrayals of what people in Okinawa have experienced since World War II came from writers of fiction and poetry. Prominent mainland novelists with such divergent political inclinations as Kawabata Yasunari (1899–1972) and Ōe Kenzaburō (b. 1935) visited the island and reported their observations. Ōe's *Okinawa nōto* (Notes on Okinawa, 1970) is a particularly incisive account of the author's personal involvement in the reversion movement and the tensions that developed between activists from Okinawa and the mainland even as they worked for a common cause. Among writers from Okinawa, poet Yamanokuchi Baku (1903–63) wrote late in his career of the prolonged American occupation and military presence in poetry and prose that brought his work to the attention of many readers on the mainland. Influential critics and editors in Tokyo also began to take notice, though somewhat belatedly, of contemporary fiction and poetry by writers from Okinawa. Perhaps the most conspicuous result of their discovery was the granting of the nation's highly coveted literary award, the Akutagawa Prize for fiction, to Ōshiro Tatsuhiro (b. 1925) for *Kakuteru pātī* (*Cocktail Party*) in 1967 and to Higashi Mineo (b. 1938) for *Okinawa no shōnen* (*Child of Okinawa*) in 1972, the year of reversion. Both works have been reissued a number of times, and the 1983 Japanese film *Okinawan Boys*, based in part on characters and episodes from Higashi's work, has played to large audiences.

Although these novellas differ sharply in tone and form, both are first-person narratives of individual protagonists whose lives are profoundly affected by the U.S. occupation and military presence. And both are distinguished for their ingenious rendering of Okinawa's lush, semitropical landscape as an often ironic backdrop to the disturbing human dramas they portray. Set in the early 1960s, *Cocktail Party* is the story of a man whose daughter is raped by an American soldier. It tells of the father's growing frustration as he struggles with the inequities of occupation law and feels the crushing impact of political realities in Okinawa on his personal relationships. *Child of Okinawa* is told through the eyes of a young adolescent growing up a decade earlier in a bar/brothel that his parents run in a town near one of the largest bases. The boy is alternately revolted and aroused by what he sees going on around him as he experiences his own confused sexual awakening. Though not without flaws, both works make for compelling reading and give considerable insight into what life is like for people whose circumstances are, far more than for most of us, beyond their ability to control. In telling the stories of their protagonists, Ōshiro and Higashi extract such experiences from the mesmerizing context of newspaper headlines and television "sound bites," bringing them to an intensely personal level that is the special realm of literature. Drawn into these individual ordeals, the reader can appreciate why it is sometimes said that fiction is truer than fact.

The two novellas are presented here in translation together with an introduction providing historical background and a concluding essay that compares and evaluates these works. The introduction is intended to supply information that will help the reader understand specific points in the stories. It concentrates on how people in Okinawa have been affected by historical events and government policies. Although motivations for Japanese and U.S. policies toward Okinawa are briefly discussed, the introduction does not seek to analyze the island's geopolitical role in international affairs. For both essays I have drawn on Japanese and English-language sources including materials collected in Okinawa during eight months of a 1967–68 overseas tour in the United States Army and on subsequent visits to the island.

Financial support for work on this project was provided by grants from the Japan Foundation, the Association for Asian Studies, and Brown University. Several people have contributed valuable advice and criticism during the preparation of the manuscript. For their assistance with the translations, I am grateful to Jo Nobuko Martin, Yuriko Saito, Etsuko Takushi, and Kikuko Yamashita for patiently answering my questions and to Gayle K. Fujita, Howard S. Hibbett, and Thomas E. Swann for their invaluable critiques of completed drafts. Special thanks go to Edward J. Drea for his expert advice and comments on the introduction and for arranging access to the archives at the United States Army Military History Institute at Carlisle Barracks, Pennsylvania, where he was assistant director. The introduction also benefited from the suggestions of Akiko Hibbett. I am grateful to Ann Berent-Johannsen for her meticulous and perceptive editing of both the translations and the essays. Furthermore, I wish to thank Kathryn A. Spicer for entering the manuscript into the appropriate computer and Joanne Sandstrom for her astute final editing. I am, of course, fully responsible for any mistakes or shortcomings that remain.

Introduction

Were half the power that fills the world with terror,
Were half the wealth bestowed on camps and courts,
Given to redeem the human mind from error,
There were no need for arsenals and forts.

"The Arsenal at Springfield"
Henry Wadsworth Longfellow, 1845

For many Japanese and Americans, Okinawa still brings to mind the last and worst battle of the Pacific War. The eighty-two days of bitter fighting with massive casualties on both sides, the kamikaze airplane attacks on American ships offshore, and the ritual suicides of Japanese senior commanders just before U.S. forces occupied the last stretch of ground on the island's southern tip in late June of 1945 are all horrifying memories of the war's final phase. In Japan, historical accounts and dramatic portrayals of these events appear regularly in print and on film. Although the Battle of Okinawa receives less attention in the United States, high school textbooks recount it at some length, and veterans who survived it are still interviewed by newspaper and television reporters at each anniversary of this murderous confrontation.[1]

Fewer Americans and Japanese outside Okinawa Prefecture remember that of the more than 230,000 who died in the fighting, over 147,000 were local residents, about one-third of the prefecture's wartime population.[2] Okinawa conscripts served and

---

[1] Members of American veterans' groups opposed the 1969 reversion agreement because they felt the United States should retain territory that was acquired at the cost of such enormous casualties.

[2] Figures cited are from Okinawa Prefectural Government, "Heiwa no ishiji" (Monument of peace) (Naha, Okinawa, 1995). (All Japanese-language sources cited herein were published in Tokyo unless otherwise indicated.)

died with the Japanese army, which fought tenaciously against advancing U.S. forces. However, thousands of civilians including children were caught in the cross fire or trapped in buildings and caves, where they were killed in machine-gun, flamethrower, and grenade attacks. Many others died when Japanese soldiers ordered mass suicides to stretch dwindling food supplies and forced civilians out of overcrowded caves into heavy enemy fire or shot them down at point-blank range.[3] When the "typhoon of steel" finally ended, almost all who survived found themselves destitute or without homes or both. Later, unknown numbers died in the aftermath of battle from exposure, unattended wounds, malnutrition, or illness.[4] If Japanese soldiers often showed little regard for the lives of local residents during the fighting, there were also reports of U.S. soldiers mistreating civilians held in refugee camps and shooting those who attempted to escape in the weeks after the Japanese defeat before American relocation and relief efforts were organized.[5]

These efforts remained makeshift and piecemeal for some time. Even after the war ended in August 1945, the scale of devastation in Okinawa and its remoteness from Supreme Allied Headquarters in Tokyo hindered the flow of relief. Nevertheless, U.S. forces made the best of what they had during the first months after the battle. They worked long hours on duty and volunteered their time off to distribute canned goods, military fatigues, medicine, cigarettes, and other supplies both as free rations and, later, to compensate for such labor as clearing war debris and driving trucks.[6] Many relief items came from large stocks brought to the island as supplies for the assault on mainland Japan that was

---

[3] Shinzato Keiji, Taminato Tomoaki, and Kinjō Seitoku, *Okinawa-ken no rekishi* (The history of Okinawa Prefecture) (Yamakawa, 1980), pp. 213–221; and Ienaga Saburō, *The Pacific War* (*Taiheiyō sensō*), translated by Frank Baldwin (New York: Pantheon, 1978), pp. 198–199. See Jo Nobuko Martin's novel *A Princess Lily of the Ryukyus* (Shin Nippon Kyōiku Tosho, 1984) for an excellent firsthand account in English of the Battle of Okinawa from the perspective of a high school student conscripted as a nurse.

[4] M. D. Morris, *Okinawa: A Tiger by the Tail* (New York: Hawthorn, 1968), p. 39; and George Kerr, *Okinawa: The History of an Island People* (Rutland, Vt.: Tuttle, 1958), p. 472. Considering Kerr's sharply critical account of the early phase of the American occupation, I cannot share the narrator's view in *Cocktail Party* that this book "was written to justify U.S. foreign policy" (see p. 37).

[5] Shinzato, Taminato, and Kinjō, p. 223. Americans I interviewed in 1985 who were stationed there shortly after the battle reported incidences of rape.

[6] Morris, pp. 55–57.

canceled after the Japanese surrender. People in Okinawa do not have pleasant memories of living in army tents, eating K-rations, and drinking powdered milk, but these early arrangements saved tens of thousands from starvation and disease.[7] Late in 1946 conditions had improved to the extent that the American military could assist in the repatriation and resettlement of more than 112,000 people to Okinawa who had been living on the mainland or in the Philippines, Saipan, and other areas formerly under Japanese control.[8]

Aside from subsistence measures, however, little was done to rehabilitate the local economy for the next three years. During this time Okinawa acquired its nickname "the rock" among American military personnel who considered it a bleak and isolated outpost. Many were "dumped" there because they had been found incompetent or unfit for duty elsewhere; and, not surprisingly, crime and corruption involving American soldiers were widespread on the island. A visit of army officials from Washington in 1949 resulted in a high-level shake-up of the local command.[9] After that Okinawa also began to receive more of the substantial economic and technological aid that was already flowing into mainland Japan and occupied areas of Western Europe. The U.S. government continued to give military needs priority, but its agencies started providing long-term assistance ranging from agricultural commodities to college scholarships. In addition, Congress allocated limited annual subsidies to the local economy for the remaining years of the occupation.

While humanitarian motives played a part in these later programs, U.S. policymakers also undertook them in Okinawa and elsewhere with a view to political and military advantages in a "postwar" world of intensifying hostilities. If the decision to invade the island in 1945 resulted from its strategic location on Japan's "southern flank," the decision four years later to rebuild the commerce and transportation infrastructure had much to do with U.S. desires for a secure bastion from which military power could be projected over a wide area of Asia. The strategic value of Okinawa under U.S. control was outlined in a report entitled

---

[7] Ibid. Also see Higa Mikio, *Politics and Parties in Postwar Okinawa* (Vancouver: University of British Columbia, 1963), p. 26, in which the author writes that "as many as 160,098 cases of malaria were reported in 1946, but this disease was gradually eradicated as a result of a U.S. public health program."

[8] Higa, p. 26.

[9] Ibid., pp. 7–8.

"The Ryukyu Islands and Their Significance" prepared by the Central Intelligence Agency for President Truman in August 1948.

1.... Possession or control of these islands, particularly Okinawa, will give the occupying country: (a) an advantage in either defensive or offensive operations in Asia; (b) a watch post to guard the sea approaches to Central and North China and Korea; and (c) a base for air surveillance over a wide area, taking Okinawa as the center.

2. U.S. control of the Ryukyu Islands would: (a) give the U.S. a position from which to operate in defense of an unarmed post-treaty Japan and U.S. bases in the Philippines and other Pacific Islands; (b) obviate the possibility of the Ryukyus falling under the control of a potential enemy; (c) neutralize, to some extent, Soviet positions in the Kuriles, Korea, and Manchuria; and (d) give the U.S. a position from which to discourage any revival of military aggression on the part of the Japanese.[10]

A year later the Joint Chiefs of Staff issued a confidential directive stating that "it is the policy of the United States to develop and maintain a substantial degree of contentment among the civil population in order to contribute to the accomplishment of military objectives."[11] Considerations of long-term military strategy were overriding, too, in the decision to retain U.S. administration of Okinawa after the Allied occupation of mainland Japan ended in 1952 and to prolong it for twenty years more. Forces were initially reduced between 1945 and 1948, but the bastion there expanded rapidly after the Chinese Communists' victory in 1949 and grew again in quantum leaps with U.S. involvement in Korea and Vietnam. Responding to criticism in Japan and elsewhere of American military rule in Okinawa, Secretary of State John Foster Dulles proclaimed that Japan held "residual sovereignty" over the Ryūkyū Islands.[12] However, three American presidents sub-

---

[10] Central Intelligence Agency, "The Ryukyu Islands and Their Significance" (August 6, 1948) (Washington, D.C.: Government Printing Office).

[11] Joint Chiefs of Staff, "Draft Directive to Commander-in-Chief, Far East for Military Government of the Ryukyu Islands," July 29, 1949, in *Foreign Relations 7* (1949): 817.

[12] Kerr, pp. 6–9. This ambiguous term had been included in Article 3 of the San Francisco Peace Treaty to characterize the status of the Ryukyus vis-à-vis Japan. Kerr subsequently notes that Dulles "unexpectedly shifted" the American position in 1956 and "broadly hinted that...the United States might have to reconsider the doctrine of 'residual sovereignty'" if Japan agreed to a peace treaty with the U.S.S.R. that conceded permanent Soviet occupation of the disputed northern islands.

sequently asserted the "military imperative" of "continuing the present status" of Okinawa "in the face of threats to peace in the Far East."[13] And one of them, John Kennedy, asked "forbearance" of the island's residents.[14]

Nothing in Okinawa's long and troubled history can match the devastation of 1945 or the scale of the military presence that has developed there since then. But efforts by outside forces to exploit the island's strategic location for military advantage go back as far as Kubilai Khan's ill-fated invasion of Japan in 1274. In those days Okinawa was an independent kingdom with a language, mythology, and social structure most closely akin to Japan's. When King Eiso refused Khan's orders to provide troops and a staging area for his planned assault, the Mongol emperor sent his forces onto the island and took Okinawan captives back to China. Fortunately, this proved to be only a temporary disturbance. Over the next three hundred years Okinawa grew prosperous, developing cultural ties and a loose tributary relationship with China as well as a flourishing trade with China, Japan, Korea, and Southeast Asia. But by the end of the sixteenth century the kingdom became increasingly caught up in a rivalry between China and Japan over, among other things, claims to suzerainty in Okinawa and control of its rich trade. In 1590 Toyotomi Hideyoshi, who had emerged from a long period of civil wars as the military overlord of Japan, ordered King Shō Nei to provide troops and supplies for Hideyoshi's planned invasion of China through Korea. After initially demurring, the king reluctantly sent food provisions to the Japanese forces, which failed to gain a foothold in Korea and withdrew after Hideyoshi's death in 1598.[15]

Though spared embroilment in a war between its neighbors, Okinawa now became an object in the conflict among warring factions in Japan over Hideyoshi's succession. When Tokugawa Ieyasu prevailed in the fighting that ended in 1600, he placed Okinawa under the domain of Shimazu Iehisa, the daimyo of Satsuma province in southern Kyūshū, as part of the settlement designed to secure Tokugawa authority over the whole country. Shimazu received the title "Lord of the Southern Islands" and in 1609 sent

---

[13] From Joint Communiqués of meetings between Prime Minister Kishi and President Eisenhower (June 11, 1957), Prime Minister Ikeda and President Kennedy (June 22, 1961), and Prime Minister Satō and President Johnson (January 13, 1965).

[14] From "Statement by the President of the United States" (March 19, 1962).

[15] Kerr, pp. 51 and 152–156; and Higa, p. 2.

an army of samurai to assert his own authority in Okinawa. Over the next two hundred years the Satsuma government imposed harsh restrictions and heavy taxes but permitted the kingdom to continue its tributary relationship with China so that the Shimazu daimyo could reap benefits from the still-flourishing trade. With the establishment of Japan's modern state after the Meiji Restoration in 1868, the kingdom was finally abolished, and Okinawa was absorbed into the Japanese body politic as a prefecture in 1879.[16]

During the last twenty years of Satsuma's authority, Okinawa was visited by naval vessels from England, France, and Russia seeking navigation, landing, and trade privileges. Fearing both the cost of such arrangements and Satsuma's displeasure, Okinawan officials denied these requests as courteously as possible. Then Commodore Matthew C. Perry arrived from the United States with a squadron of battleships in 1853. Perry's mission sought not only the right of "sale and barter," but also permission for "the occupation of the principal ports of those islands for the accommodation of our ships of war." Perry also saw Okinawa as a potential bargaining chip if difficulties arose in his efforts to negotiate a treaty of navigation and trade with Japan. He appealed to his superiors in Washington for approval to seize Okinawa as an American "protectorate." He warned that "I should have instructions to act promptly, for it is not impossible that some other power, less scrupulous, may slip in and seize upon the advantages which should justly belong to us." And he claimed that, in any case, such drastic action was "justified by the strictist rules of moral law" considering "the grinding oppression of their [Satsuma] rulers."[17] President Franklin Pierce's advisors promptly rejected what they called Perry's "embarrassing... suggestion." He was told that the president "is disinclined... to take and retain possession of an island in that distant country" in view of "mortifying" choices the United States might face "if resistance should be offered and threatened."[18] Though thwarted, Perry's plans to occupy Okinawa and build a naval base there foreshadowed what happened a century later, after World War II, not only because they were inspired by Okinawa's strategic location and a desire to

---

[16] Kerr, pp. 157–169.

[17] From letters of Commodore Perry to the Secretary of the Navy dated December 14, 1852; December 24, 1852; and January 25, 1854. Quoted in Kerr, pp. 305 and 327.

[18] From letter of the Secretary of the Navy to Commodore Perry dated May 30, 1854. Quoted in Kerr, pp. 327–328.

preempt what were thought to be other powers' designs, but also because they were "justified" as beneficial to the island's residents, who had suffered under Japanese rule.

As Supreme Allied Commander during the occupation of Japan, General Douglas MacArthur emphasized that Okinawa's strategic location made it "absolutely necessary" that the United States "retain unilateral and complete control."[19] However, unlike President Pierce's advisors, U.S. military and intelligence officials seemed little concerned in the late 1940s that Okinawa residents might object to such control. In a conversation reported by George Kennan in 1948, General MacArthur characterized them as "simple and good-natured people" who, having been "looked down on" by Japanese, could now "pick up a good deal of money and have a reasonably happy existence from an American base development."[20]

MacArthur was evidently informed of the discrimination that people from Okinawa had experienced in mainland Japan. And military construction did provide spin-off income for the island's devastated economy during the early years after World War II. But his statements revealed a condescending attitude that was also expressed with unabashed candor by military commanders who later administered the occupation of Okinawa.[21] Perhaps after seeing people in a state of destitution who thankfully accepted relief and such jobs as were offered them, U.S. officials were deluded into thinking that local residents would always be grateful for American "protection" and for the kind of livelihoods offered by a military-service economy. Widely held stereotypes of a "simple" and easily accommodated people also help explain why many in the U.S. military refused for so long to believe that growing demands for reduction of the bases and reversion to

---

[19] "Conversation between General of the Army MacArthur and Mr. George F. Kennan, March 5, 1948," in *Foreign Relations* 6 (1948): 701. General MacArthur's remarks are recounted by Mr. Kennan.

[20] Ibid.

[21] Former commanders of the American occupation of Okinawa stated their opinions in wide-ranging interviews conducted in the 1970s by the U.S. Army Military History Institute as part of the institute's Senior Officers Debriefing Program. In the transcript of an interview on April 21, 1975, Lieutenant General Paul W. Caraway refers to people in Okinawa as "countrified" (Conversation no. 12, p. 7), "tiny little people" (p. 38), and "you boys" (p. 59). Discussing local businesses in his interview of April 29, 1975, Lieutenant General Ferdinand T. Unger said of people in Okinawa that "they just didn't know how to run things" (p. 9) and "they were like babes in the woods" (p. 10).

Japanese sovereignty represented genuine popular opinion on the island.[22] Higa Mikio, a political scientist from Okinawa, wrote in 1963 about the risks of such misperceptions.

> The description of Okinawans as a docile and submissive people, so frequently used by foreign observers, is not without truth. Undoubtedly it comes in part from the long history of having to interact with stronger peoples around them.... But to assume that the basic interests and instincts of this "docile" people can be ignored is to court trouble, as has been discovered by the United States several times in the recent past.[23]

One of the first jobs Americans offered people in Okinawa after the Japanese surrender was collecting the enormous stores of weapons and ammunition brought there for the assault on mainland Japan that never took place. Much of this matériel was then shipped to Chiang Kai-shek's forces, who were fighting the Communists in China. After Chiang's defeat, military construction in Okinawa shifted into high gear. The United States was theoretically at peace, but a major conflict of interservice rivalries broke out as units of the U.S. Army, Navy, and Marines vied to build installations outdoing one another in size and comfort on their own chosen sectors of the island.[24] Local environmental conditions, particularly frequent typhoons and the lack of deep-water bays, forced the scaling down of plans for a major naval base, but work went ahead on hundreds of other projects. These included installations for launching aircraft, storing weapons, gathering intelligence, and training troops as well as housing and recreation facilities. A number of people impoverished by the battle and its aftermath found employment on these projects or as maids and service workers on the expanding bases. But for many more, base construction meant the sacrifice of their lands and livelihoods to military exigencies.

The expansion of the American bases also gave birth to a sharply bifurcated society on the island. While thousands in Okinawa were still living from day to day in borrowed shelter and eating imported staples, officers clubs and mess halls on the other side of high wire fences sported tablecloths and real silverware. Meals were served there by Philippine stewards in elegant white uniforms, and premium brand Scotch sold for ten cents a glass.[25]

---

[22] Higa, pp. 8–9 and 91–92.
[23] Ibid., pp. 91–92.
[24] Morris, p. 61.
[25] Ibid.

With the massive influx of U.S. military and civilian personnel during the Korean War, American, mainland Japanese, and local contractors hired Okinawa residents to build not only headquarters buildings, ammunition depots, and hospitals, but also tennis courts, golf courses, swimming pools, baseball and football fields, bowling alleys, commissaries, schools, and thousands of family housing units in what soon became known as "permbase," the largest complex of American military facilities outside the United States. By the mid-1950s desperate post-battle conditions were a thing of the past, but poverty was still widespread among local residents living outside the American enclaves. A decade later the population of U.S. personnel and their families was approaching 80,000, and "dependent housing areas" were beginning to resemble modest suburbs in the American sunbelt. After years when Okinawa was considered a hardship assignment, these facilities made the island's old GI nickname "the rock" into an ironic anachronism.

To secure space for the bases and their surrounding enclaves, occupation authorities drafted ordinances in 1950 and 1952 that authorized the "renting" at a set rate of what were often valuable tracts of cultivated farm land. To call this "renting" was deceptive, first, because once covered with pavement, tarmac, or gravel, such land—already in short supply—could not be returned to agricultural use.[26] Second, no one could refuse to rent his land. Higa Mikio described the consequences of this policy.

> By the very nature of its economy and due to the lack of natural resources, Okinawa is predominantly agricultural. To the Okinawans, land is the most cherished possession, as it is the sole means of livelihood to most of them. Their attachment to the land is very strong, and voluntary sales are not common. It is difficult for a dispossessed farmer to obtain substitute land or change his occupation.[27]

Evacuation orders led to strenuous protests and to criticism in the United States from the American Civil Liberties Union.[28] Land seizures sparked some of the earliest mass demonstrations against U.S. authorities in Okinawa. At several sites large groups of

---

[26] Kerr, p. 6.

[27] Higa, p. 41.

[28] Higashimatsu Teruaki, *Okinawa ni kichi ga aro* (Bases in Okinawa) (Gurabia Seikō Sha, 1969), pp. 64–67; and Akio Watanabe, *The Okinawa Problem: A Chapter in Japan-U.S. Relations* (Melbourne, Australia: Melbourne University Press, 1970), pp. 139–140.

farmers sat down in front of bulldozers defying repeated warnings until forcibly removed by American troops carrying carbines and tear gas.[29] These local protests in the early 1950s were the forerunners of larger rallies in the 1960s organized to express public sentiment on a variety of issues. Occupation authorities responded to the furor over land by promising to negotiate with local residents in individual cases. But protests broke out again in 1954 when the U.S. Army publicly announced that it intended to make lump-sum payments to landowners for use of their properties into the indefinite future. After four more years of negotiations and lengthy congressional hearings, the issue was defused somewhat by the announcement of a revised policy in 1958 that increased rental payments to rates that would be reevaluated every five years.[30] Although the dreaded lump-sum proposal had been scrapped, the new policy offered little to small landowners who had farmed their own fields for generations. Lacking education and marketable skills, many of them turned for their livelihoods to the GI bar business or other base-town enterprises.

Land seizure was only one of many ways the prolonged American occupation and military presence impinged on the lives of Okinawa residents and became a festering sore in U.S.-Japanese relations. When the San Francisco Peace Treaty released the rest of the country from occupation rule in 1952, resentment in Okinawa was hardly assuaged by U.S. assertions that the island was better off not rejoining Japan. For people in Okinawa, September 8, 1951, the date of the treaty's signing, became known as a "day of shame."[31] Anger was directed at both Washington and Tokyo for "selling out" Okinawa, relegating it to an indeterminate future under foreign control so that the mainland could regain its sovereignty. The agreement was seen by many as an extension of the Japanese government's discriminatory policy toward Okinawa Prefecture between 1879 and 1945, when people there paid higher taxes and received fewer social services than anywhere else in the country. Aware of this policy and of Okinawa's earlier history of harsh and exploitative control by Satsuma, American officials widely echoed General MacArthur's view that, especially in the economic sphere, Okinawa would benefit more under U.S. military occupation than it would by returning to Japanese sovereignty.

[29] Higashimatsu, pp. 66–67.
[30] Higa, pp. 40–56.
[31] Shinzato, Taminato, and Kinjō, pp. 223–226.

And many Americans expressed the opinion that in the future, people there should seek permanent affiliation with the United States or some other political status independent of Japan. Even when opinion polls and election results later showed overwhelming sentiment favoring reversion and a reduction of the military presence, U.S. officials tended to dismiss these views and a broadly based reversion movement as the products of leftist agitation.[32]

Americans could be proud of the role U.S. forces had played in Okinawa's recovery from post-battle devastation. However, those who touted the material benefits of the continuing military presence too often ignored the long-term problems it brought. They also exaggerated the role of the bases in bringing a higher standard of living to Okinawa than prevailed in most other areas of East Asia (excluding, significantly, mainland Japan). By the early 1950s the U.S. government was paying wages to some 50,000 local residents employed in construction, maintenance, and service jobs on the bases. But an economy centered on such jobs, which had little attraction for young people with education and skills, could not be called productive.[33] Nor could the "prosperity" often referred to by American officials be considered stable when it relied heavily on foreign subsidies and the daily purchases of off-duty military personnel.

It was a sad irony for people in Okinawa that the continuing occupation and vast military presence prolonged economic dependence on the projects and purchases of American forces. Considering the still-depressed conditions of mainland Japan at the time of the San Francisco Peace Treaty, it is difficult to project with

---

[32] Higa, pp. 8–9 and 91–92. Higa cites a petition signed by 199,000 eligible voters (72.1 percent of the total) favoring reversion in mid-1951 and estimates that some 90 percent favored reversion by the early 1960s. He also concedes that "a few Okinawans (and a number of Americans) have supported the idea of independence" and that "a small number of Okinawans...have advocated United Nations Trusteeship either with the United States as sole administering authority or with the United States and Japan as joint administrators." Detailed results of opinion polls on reversion and the U.S. military presence are published in Ryūkyū Shinpō Sha, ed., *Kichi Okinawa* (Okinawa's bases) (Simul, 1968), pp. 222–276. A capsule history of the reversion movement is given in Watanabe, pp. 135–149.

[33] Mainland companies and government agencies with contracts in Okinawa faced a shortage of skilled workers after reversion because so many young people had left Okinawa to find employment on the mainland and elsewhere during the occupation years. Many firms hired workers from other prefectures despite the added expense of bringing them to the island.

precision how Okinawa would have fared economically over the next twenty years had it reverted to Japanese sovereignty with a reduced military presence in 1952. But post-treaty actions of the government in Tokyo suggest that Okinawa as a Japanese prefecture would have benefited from the country's spectacular economic growth beginning in the early 1960s. As it was, the Japanese government gave increasing financial assistance to Okinawa annually, surpassing direct American monetary aid by 1965, and granted preferential tariffs that stimulated sales on the mainland of Okinawan sugar and pineapples, produced by sectors of the local economy with little or no connection to the military.[34]

More important, those who emphasized the material benefits of the bases too often failed to consider the quality of life in Okinawa. Few residents could escape the effects of living in a place where the activities of military forces posed frequent inconveniences and not uncommon risks, where ultimate political and judicial authority rested with the general of a foreign army, and where the economy of certain areas depended almost entirely on the leisure spending of thousands of soldiers, sailors, and marines. U.S. officials who lived in the residential enclaves as privileged members of Okinawa's bifurcated society consistently downplayed the dangers, disruptions, and injustices encountered by local residents. And Japanese or U.S. reporters who wrote about them were labeled troublemakers by the high command. Even M. D. Morris, a former army officer whose book *Okinawa: Tiger by the Tail* (1967) supported the continued military presence and opposed reversion, acknowledged the grim reality of the bases for those in Okinawa living outside the American enclaves at the height of the Vietnam War.

> Throughout the island's countryside, U.S. war machines dominate the landscape. Huge aircraft, small aircraft, and helicopters fill the sky day and night, and high-tension towers transmitting megawatts of electric power via scores of cables loom overhead like puppet lines of giant skeleton scarecrows.
>
> Mountains of systematically stacked chemical drums and wood

---

[34] Okinawan cement also sold well on the mainland. General Unger provides the aid figures in his interview of April 29, 1975 (p. 5). During the early 1960s the American military actually insisted that the Japanese government stop increasing its aid to Okinawa for fear that, if it exceeded American aid, the United States would "lose face." See Edwin O. Reischauer, *My Life between Japan and America* (New York: Harper and Row, 1986), p. 204. Former ambassador Reischauer notes here that "fortunately we were able in time to get rid of this ridiculous strategy."

shipping crates range over square miles of depot areas fenced in by mesh and barbed wire. Acres of new vehicles sticky with cosmoline stand ready to be put into motion in convoy caravans. Tanks and amphibious vehicles wait in port areas, where fleets of ships daily bring more military stores for stacking, then take away from those same stacks for distribution and destruction in Viet Nam. Radio antennae fields stand along the shore, while radar and missile sites mushroom in the hills.

On the ground, giant steel pipelines carry endless gallons of diesel oil, jet fuel, lube oil, gasoline, and fresh water to thousands of machines. And stored below ground in massive shockproof, radiation-proof, fireproof steel and concrete caverns, are reservoirs of petroleum products; magazines with megadeaths of munitions; and the billionth-of-a-second sensitive computerized control centers, the brain and nerve cells of this island bastion.

At many combat training areas in the north, jungle and village battle situations are simulated with deadly precision. Near the coast, periodic live-missile firing drills keep the troops alert—and their neighbors alarmed.[35]

People living or traveling near the bases have not been the only ones with reason to feel apprehensive. Crashes of military aircraft, including a jet fighter that fell on a school in 1959 killing 17 and injuring 121, continue to take their toll more than fifteen years after reversion.[36] Many more civilians have died or been maimed every year in numerous traffic accidents involving both official vehicles operated by military personnel and private cars driven by U.S. forces or their dependents. Some accidents have involved tanks and trucks carrying high explosives. In July 1969 a leak of poison gas, stored in large quantities in Okinawa at the time, caused widespread alarm.[37] Wayward artillery and mortar shells from combat exercises still fall on the outskirts of towns, sometimes starting fires.[38] Leakages of gasoline and jet fuel from storage tanks on the bases have poisoned wells and polluted farm fields. Noise from the constant traffic of fighter, bomber, and

---

[35] Morris, pp. 2–3.

[36] Watanabe, pp. 65–66; and Shinzato, Taminato, and Kinjō, p. 241. A fully loaded B-52 bomber crashed near an ammunition depot in November 1968. The prefectural government reports 115 accidents of military aircraft between 1972 and 1995. Also see Preface, p. x.

[37] Ryūkyū Shinpō Sha, pp. 138–140; Shimabukuro Kazuya, *Fukki-go no Okinawa* (Okinawa after reversion) (Kyōikusha, 1979), pp. 108–110; and Shinzato, Taminato, and Kinjō, p. 242.

[38] Shimabukuro, p. 110.

transport planes has damaged the hearing and disrupted the lives of people living near military runways.[39] And ultrapowerful transmitters for the Voice of America have caused bizarre accidents in which appliances in private homes have suddenly caught fire and livestock have been felled by electric shocks. In addition, the number of crimes committed by military personnel, mostly younger enlisted men, against Okinawa residents rose sharply when the island became a base for U.S. combat operations.[40] Beyond apprehensions raised by these incidents is a more generalized fear among people all too familiar with the horrors of war that Okinawa, widely believed to be a staging area for U.S. nuclear weapons, could once again come under attack.[41]

Aside from physical hazards posed by the bases, Okinawa residents bore the political, social, and psychological consequences of foreign military occupation twenty years longer than mainland Japan despite occasional efforts to soften them. Higa Mikio wrote in 1963 that "one of the principal criticisms of the American administration is its continued military character."[42] Edwin O. Reischauer, U.S. ambassador to Japan from 1961 to 1966 and an early U.S. advocate of reversion, recalled in 1977 that "American military rule" with its "alienness and arrogance... only grudgingly opened the way to local autonomy."[43]

The various civilian offices and agencies created during the occupation could never obscure the reality of a territory controlled by military organizations, which are authoritarian by nature and have scant experience in civil management.[44] Limited efforts to restore autonomy began in 1945 when a U.S. "Military Government" (M.G.) conducted local elections and delegated authority over routine matters to community leaders. In 1950 a "U.S. Civil Administration of the Ryukyu Islands" (USCAR) was set up under the military command to implement American policies and programs. Two years later the United States created a "Government

---

[39] Ibid.

[40] Crimes by U.S. personnel against local civilians: 973 in 1964, 1,003 in 1965, 1,407 in 1966. Atrocious and violent crimes: 265 in 1964, 275 in 1965, 466 in 1966. Figures in Watanabe, p. 65.

[41] Arasaki Moriteru, *Sengo Okinawa-shi* (Postwar Okinawan history) (Nihon Hyōron Sha, 1982), pp. 300–304; Shinzato, Taminato, and Kinjō, p. 235; Watanabe, pp. 66–67; and opinion surveys in Ryūkyū Shinpō Sha, pp. 229–230.

[42] Higa, p. 35.

[43] Edwin O. Reischauer, *The Japanese* (Tokyo: Tuttle, 1977), p. 348.

[44] Higa, p. 35.

of the Ryukyu Islands" (G.R.I.) composed of a legislature and a "Chief Executive" who was appointed at first by the U.S. military from among local leaders and later chosen by the legislature subject to U.S. approval. For twenty years the G.R.I. operated the bus lines, postal service, certain civilian courts, and other public services. The army lieutenant general commanding the occupation, however, whose title of "High Commissioner" carried the unfortunate ring of British colonialism, retained the ultimate power.

High commissioners could and did force elected officials from office, block G.R.I. legislation, and overrule the judgments of G.R.I. courts. In practice, these men preferred the application of economic and political pressures behind the scenes to outright vetoes and firings, but the results were the same. Such pressures led to the removal in 1957 of the mayor of Naha, elected the previous year,[45] and to the defeat in 1962 of a redistricting bill passed by the G.R.I. legislature that would have created electoral districts in Okinawa with approximately equal numbers of eligible voters.[46] High commissioners also had final authority over transportation, investment, education, and such lifeline sources as water, fuel, and electric power. Interviewed in 1971, Lieutenant General Paul W. Caraway described his powers as high commissioner and his relations with USCAR and the G.R.I. during his term from 1961 to 1964.

> *Interviewer:* What did the office of High Commissioner...equate to?
> *General Caraway:* Well, I don't know what it equated to, but as far as what you could do, you stood about halfway between being president and the governor of a state. In other words, nobody said you "nay" on any subject. Locally, nobody said you "nay." I could veto any legislation that passed, if I couldn't block it before they passed it.... And I could—if they wouldn't pass legislation required or if I had to get legislation passed or something changed—I could issue an ordnance [sic] a High Commissioner's ordnance [sic] which was a law. It was promulgated and proclaimed, and it became the law of the Ryukyu Islands.... I could remove people from office if they gave cause for it. In the High Commissioner resided fifty percent of the stock of the Bank of the Ryukyus, which was the central bank. I could shut down an insurance business, or any other business...I could keep people out and I could let them in.

---

[45] Watanabe, pp. 157–158. Mayor Senaga Kamejirō's removal from office was called colonialism in the Japanese press.

[46] Higa, p. 85.

Interviewer: Then you had practically absolute governing power?
General Caraway: Well, that's what everybody liked to say. They
made a despot of you. But I had all the authority that anybody
needed to operate the Ryukyu Islands, and I used it....
Interviewer: What's this USCAR?
General Caraway: United States Civil Administration Ryukyu Islands,
USCAR, which was my staff. They had gotten so that nobody ever
remembered the High Commissioner.... Of course, that's the first
thing I changed. I said, "I'm the locus of power, and I'm going to
exercise the power. Now, you people who've been thinking you've
been running an operation, and that you were the government of
the Ryukyu Islands, you may as well find out that you aren't." It
took quite some doing. They didn't want to bow to me, but the
Ryukyuians [*sic*] convinced them. Because as soon as the Ryukyuians [*sic*] found out that I was highly visible, and what I said went,
and if I said no, it stopped dead, they paid little attention to
USCAR after that, except for routine stuff. The rest of the time they
came to me.[47]

General Caraway and the other five men who held the office of
high commissioner approved funding for such worthwhile projects
as building water-filtration plants and schools and purchasing ath-
letic equipment for students. However, when deciding issues that
affected both the lives of local residents and the operation of the
bases, they too often opted for massive overreaction, even when
the potential for inconvenience to the military mission seemed
extremely remote. Particularly troubling to people in Okinawa
were restrictions maintained on (1) travel to and from the mainland (investigations and passports required), (2) imports of capital
(prohibited without special licenses), and (3) labor unions (no col-
lective bargaining for base workers). Over the years a number of
students who passed entrance examinations for mainland colleges
lost their rights to admission because of delays in processing their
passports. And there were people with critically ill family
members on the mainland who were unable to secure passports
when needed. Workers picketing in towns near the bases were
met by lines of police or, on occasion, by MPs armed with rifles
and fixed bayonets.[48] In some cases, high commissioners could
probably have avoided demonstrations and bad publicity had they
not insisted on enforcing such dubious occupation measures as

---

[47] Interview of April 21, 1975, pp. 17–21.
[48] American authorities preferred to use local police, but MPs were dispatched
during a number of demonstrations in the 1960s.

those restricting the political activities of school teachers and prohibiting display of the Japanese flag except on national holidays.[49] The command also might have been more responsive to complaints about shortages of water for civilian use and traffic problems resulting from priority passage of military vehicles on the roads.

Perhaps the most disturbing aspect of this system of dual but unequal authority concerned legal jurisdiction. A special division of courts within USCAR exercised superiority over G.R.I. courts and was empowered to try and to sentence local civilians in any case deemed appropriate by the high commissioner. Furthermore, occupation law specified punishments, including execution, for Okinawa residents convicted in these courts of crimes against U.S. military personnel or their dependents.[50] On the other hand, no civil or criminal court of the G.R.I. had the power to try as defendants or summon as witnesses U.S. military personnel in cases of crimes committed against local civilians. In practice, American defendants rarely were prosecuted vigorously in courts martial and often received comparatively light sentences even after pleading guilty to serious offenses. Many cases were simply shelved by the military, with no action taken. Such legal inequities result in the dilemma of the father who seeks to press charges against his daughter's assailant in the novella *Cocktail Party*.

Among actual cases, one that stirred bitter resentment arose in 1963 from the death of a middle school boy run over by a truck driven by a U.S. marine. Witnesses testified that the boy had been crossing the street at a designated crosswalk on a green light in the middle of the afternoon. And the defendant himself conceded that the light had been green. Yet he was acquitted of responsibility by a court martial because he testified that the reflection of the sunlight had obstructed his view of the traffic signal.[51] Later cases in which American military personnel were involved in the deaths or injuries of local residents sparked large protest rallies. In May 1970 a girl on her way home from high school was knifed and seriously wounded by a U.S. soldier in an apparent rape attempt. Only after hundreds of people from her village staged demonstra-

---

[49] Arasaki, pp. 271–290. In mid-1968, one year before announcement of a reversion agreement, General Unger recognized Zengunrō (Union of Military Employees) as negotiating agent for workers on the bases.

[50] The vast majority of cases in which civilians were charged with crimes against the American military involved the pilfering of U.S. government property.

[51] Ryūkyū Shinpō Sha, pp. 138–140.

tions in front of his army unit and sat down en masse at USCAR headquarters in Naha was the suspect placed under arrest. Later, the press reported that growing public outcry had thwarted the army's plans for his hasty reassignment off the island.[52]

The number of robberies, assaults, and murders in which the victims were taxi drivers, waitresses, or others whose jobs brought them into contact with military personnel increased sharply during U.S. involvement in Vietnam.[53] Local police complained that, even in cases when evidence strongly implicated Americans, suspects would be absorbed back into their units and later transferred out of the command without any indication of their having been arrested or tried.[54] Growing frustration led to the forming of human rights advocacy groups in Okinawa within the reversion movement. Local leaders particularly noted the contradiction between American ideals of equality under the law and the disposition of criminal cases on the island. Fukuchi Hiroaki, director of one human rights organization, spoke of psychological as well as legal ramifications of the problem.

> Incidents of Americans shoplifting or running off without paying restaurant bills and taxi fares are now occurring daily. To the perpetrators these may seem like trivial matters, but for those who are victimized the situation has become intolerable. Though I regret to say it, there seems to be a feeling among these Americans that, as occupiers of Okinawa, they have committed no crime. And the

---

[52] Makise Tsuneji, *Okinawa no rekishi* (History of Okinawa), vol. 3 (Chōbunsha, 1971), pp. 185–195.

[53] Figures cited in Ryūkyū Shinpō Sha, pp. 134–138.

[54] Ibid., pp. 139–141. Crimes committed by Americans against Americans also increased sharply during the Vietnam War. Interunit rivalries, especially among marines, led to beatings and at least one murder. And racial tensions, acutely disturbing to the military command, heightened even as the U.S. armed forces publicized their intentions to end unofficial discrimination and equalize opportunities among all personnel. Widespread fighting broke out on several occasions in the late 1960s in a section of Koza City (renamed Okinawa City after reversion) filled with GI bars. The worst incident occurred in 1968 when fist fights between white and black troops brought squads of MPs into the area who clashed sporadically with rock-throwing enlisted men for several hours. After each disturbance, the U.S. high command made strenuous efforts to defuse a situation that could have seriously disrupted military operations in Okinawa. These efforts included personal visits by the high commissioner and his senior staff officers to Koza that were intended to promote goodwill. Generals Lampert and Maples made it a special point to stop at bars in an area of Koza where the clientele were predominantly black Americans.

code and enforcement of criminal laws here only fuels this attitude.[55]

Crimes against local residents, the suspected presence of nuclear weapons, and the deployment of B-52s, which began direct bombing missions to Southeast Asia in 1965, were the three issues provoking the most intense opposition to the American occupation and military presence in Okinawa. Japanese and American observers agree that, if reversion had not finally been negotiated in 1969, this opposition would have begun to jeopardize the U.S. military mission. The B-52s, called "sky murderers" and "black killer planes" in Okinawa, symbolized U.S. involvement in Vietnam that was staged in large part from bases on the island.[56] People there and on the mainland tended to sympathize with the victims of U.S. bombings and to identify American intervention in Southeast Asia with Japan's earlier acts of destruction in China.[57]

Large demonstrations against the B-52s and the Vietnam War in Okinawa were disruptive, though rarely violent. However, a full-fledged riot erupted a few blocks from the largest U.S. air force base in December 1970 after a local pedestrian was injured in an accident with a car driven by an American soldier. Accounts of this incident vary. According to witnesses, the driver of the car was quickly released by the MPs, while the victim was left unattended in the street.[58] American officials maintained that the pedestrian had been intoxicated and that, in any case, his injuries turned out not to be serious.[59] But whatever the circumstances of the accident, it was followed that night by crowds of people rampaging through the streets around the base for several hours. They threw rocks at the MPs and burned all cars in their path carrying the special "Keystone of the Pacific" license plates issued to U.S. forces for their private vehicles. Several people broke into the base and set fire to the air force personnel office and the American school. This brought five hundred armed troops firing tear gas grenades, but order was not restored until after seven o'clock the next morning.[60]

---

[55] Ryūkyū Shinpō Sha, p. 139.

[56] Shinzato, Taminato, and Kinjō, pp. 239–242.

[57] Reischauer, *The Japanese*, p. 347.

[58] Shinzato, Taminato, and Kinjō, p. 243.

[59] Colonel William Schless stated in his Senior Officers Debriefing Interview of January 7, 1975, that the "inebriated pedestrian, an Okinawan," had been "drunk, lying in the street" and "was not badly hurt" (p. 3).

[60] Gibe Keishun, Aniya Masaaki, and Kurima Yasuo, *Sengo Okinawa no rekishi*

Although sparked by one incident, the length and ferocity of this disturbance suggest that it resulted from frustrations that had been building for some time. Shortly before the riot political scientist Akio Watanabe wrote, "United States leaders probably saw a danger, from recent developments in Okinawa, that the rising dissatisfaction of the Okinawan people might jeopardize the smooth operation of the military bases unless a timely solution was made."[61] And former ambassador Reischauer confirmed that the U.S. government agreed to make concessions during the reversion negotiations in part out of concern that "irredentist feelings in Okinawa would probably undermine the utility of the bases there."[62] Thus, ironically, the prolonged occupation that was intended to ensure unrestricted use of U.S. installations had now become a liability to their continued operation.

Although far less likely to grab headlines or spark mass demonstrations, the stifling economic effects of the vast military presence in Okinawa also caused resentment. Those who praised the material benefits generated by the bases too often failed to consider the kind of enterprises commonly created in a military-service economy. The sad truth is that these businesses are frequently of a low-capital, nonproductive nature and tend to discourage the development of healthier, more productive industries. Furthermore, some among them, such as "the world's oldest profession," can actually have a negative effect on the community. What happened to sections of certain towns in postwar Okinawa, officially known as "amusement areas," is not unlike what happened to parts of Frankfurt, West Germany, and Juarez, Mexico, or to Columbia, South Carolina, San Diego, California, and other cities adjacent to large military bases in the United States. One city on the island, Koza, became so notorious for its GI bar and brothel district that its name was changed after reversion.[63] M. D. Morris gives a description from the mid-1960s of another such district in Naha, Okinawa's capital, better known for its many historical sites, attractive shops, and quiet residential neighborhoods.[64]

(Postwar history of Okinawa) (Nihon Seinen Shuppansha, 1971), pp. 274–278.

[61] Watanabe, p. 72.

[62] Reischauer, *The Japanese,* p. 349.

[63] To Okinawa-shi (Okinawa City). See n. 54. Koza's "amusement area" is the setting for the novella *Child of Okinawa* (see pp. 79–117), narrated by an adolescent boy growing up there.

[64] At this time there was another brothel district in Naha catering to local clientele.

Incongruously in the area surrounding the Nami-No-Ue shrine, there abounds block after block of nothing but bar after bawdy bar. Historically, Nami-No-Ue was a shrine at which arrivals and departures of distinguished travelers were celebrated in ancient times. Also enshrined there is a sacred phosphorescent stone supposedly picked up in a fisherman's net in Naha harbor ages ago. There is a Shinto shrine building at the top of the stairs. Behind a second gate and off to the right is a Buddhist temple surrounded by bells and appropriate small shrines. The annual celebration on Adults Day, shortly before the Lunar New Year's, is held there. This is the day when people go up in fancy costumes to decorate the shrine.... Annually a hundred thousand people have to pick their way through all kinds of Americanized night clubs and whorehouses in order to get to a religious shrine celebration. This is one of the enigmas of Okinawa.... And because so much money is involved in the area, nothing is going to alter this condition.

I was amazed as I wandered through this neon-lit nirvana for Neanderthals at the number of establishments, some even boasting the "A" sign of military approval.... On any given night the routine is the same. Armed forces jeeps at the ready patrol the streets, which teem with enlisted service personnel of all branches... in and out of uniforms. Pawnshops interspersed in the blocks break the monotony of bar doors. Whenever some GI runs out of ready cash, he can always go next door and hock his watch or bracelet. Occasionally, if a boy has spent enough on drinks and pays a girl's "out fee," the two may then retire to one of the "hotels" in the area, after which he will sweat out the next two weeks hoping he hasn't gotten VD.[65]

The selling of sex to American servicemen in Okinawa was actually organized and regulated by the U.S. Military Government (unofficially, of course) for a brief time in 1946. Disturbed by increasing instances of rape against civilian women, the command operated a bus service to a designated area where local prostitutes were permitted to ply their trade regulated through medical examinations, set fees, and controlled sale of alcoholic beverages. Pressure from military chaplains and the growth of unregulated prostitution outside the designated location, however, spelled an early end to this project.[66] Thereafter, prostitution became so widespread in the booming "amusement areas" of towns near the bases that, during the Vietnam build-up, it was believed to account for the largest off-base "consumer" expenditure by military personnel.

---

[65] Morris, p. 102.
[66] Ibid., pp. 60–61.

Far from providing a safe outlet for soldiers and marines carrying
several months of combat pay on short-term leaves from Vietnam,
however, unregulated prostitution is known to have resulted in
sharply higher incidences of venereal disease, black marketeering,
and violent crime.[67] Perhaps its saddest victims were young
women, some in their teens, who undertook or prolonged careers
as prostitutes after they or members of their families had incurred
debts to unscrupulous moneylenders who would threaten and
inflict physical harm when payments were late.[68]

Considering the many destructive consequences of occupation
and militarization in Okinawa, it is perhaps surprising that viru-
lent anti-Americanism of the kind seen in parts of Latin America
and the Middle East never caught on there. Ambivalent feelings
expressed toward the United States seemed to derive in part from
anxieties about mainland attitudes and intentions stemming from
Okinawa's earlier experience as a Japanese prefecture. Polls
showed that, as the U.S. occupation dragged on, more and more
people became convinced of the necessity for returning to
Japanese sovereignty.[69] But memories were still fresh of outrageous wartime sacrifices imposed on Okinawa residents by the
Japanese army and of prewar neglect by a government that allocated meager resources to its poorest prefecture. Many could also
recall suffering personal discrimination in prewar Japan, where
people who gave Okinawa as their home address were sometimes
refused employment and denied lodging. Then, after the war,
Okinawa was barely mentioned in mainland schoolbooks, and
misconceptions abounded among younger Japanese, who would
ask people from Okinawa if they spoke English at home or used
knives and forks for their daily meals. Even during the long campaign for reversion, local residents complained that mainland
Japanese tended to think not of liberating their fellow countrymen
from foreign occupation, but of regaining territory lost in war.
Many were also disappointed because they felt that opposition

---

[67] The Army's 2nd Logistical Command reported in late 1967 that strains of venereal disease from Southeast Asia resistant to antibiotics were spreading among
U.S. forces in Okinawa. Subsequently, boxes of condoms were placed next to
sign-out sheets in the orderly rooms of all units. Military personnel engaged in
such shady enterprises as drug dealing and the sale of military-issue handguns
from post armories and meat from mess-hall kitchens to local buyers.

[68] The protagonist's father in *Child of Okinawa* explains how women working in
bars were lured into debt (see p. 86).

[69] See opinion poll results in Ryūkyū Shinpō Sha, pp. 222–276.

political parties on the mainland were simply using "the Okinawa issue" as a political football to attack the conservative party that controlled the government. And there were, of course, more practical concerns because, for better or worse, much of Okinawa's economy was linked to U.S. expenditures, and people feared disruptions that might occur when it was integrated more fully into the Japanese economy. The island's special trade status—which included a tax-free port of transit and high tariffs on selected imports—protected local businesses from competition with huge and powerful conglomerates on the mainland.[70]

Beyond worries over mainland attitudes and intentions, ambivalent feelings toward the United States also resulted because the effects of the U.S. presence were by no means entirely negative. Economic aid and locally contracted development projects were obvious benefits. Aside from military facilities, the United States funded the construction of many public roads and buildings, including the University of the Ryukyus, called Okinawa's first college since no institution of higher education had been established there previously by the Japanese government. But on a deeper level people who opposed U.S. occupation and military policies on the one hand could also admire aspects of American culture available to them on the island. Official efforts to promote goodwill had some effect in this regard. U.S. funds helped to build and staff "Ryūkyū-American Friendship Centers" in several towns where libraries of books and films from the United States were available. People came even from remote rural areas to attend presentations at the centers and to study English conversation. Less successful were such campaigns as the army's "people-to-people" program, in which local mayors and business leaders were invited to clubs on the bases to join army officers and their wives in celebrating such U.S. holidays as Thanksgiving and the Fourth of July. Even generous outlays of food and liquor never seemed to bring the two groups together over the language barrier and the mutual feelings of awkwardness on these occasions; in fact, such events actually heightened resentment over the comparatively opulent American lifestyle.

As one might expect, people have learned much more about the United States through the unofficial media of books,

---

[70] Asahi Shinbun Sha, ed., *Okinawa hōkoku* (Reports from Okinawa) (Asahi Shinbun Sha, 1969). Portions are translated in *Japan Interpreter* 6 (Autumn 1970): 294–308.

newspapers, magazines, movies, radio, and television. During the occupation there was a U.S. commercial radio station in Okinawa as well as U.S. forces radio and television channels. A daily newspaper, the *Okinawa Morning Star*, was published in English, and magazines from the United States were cheaper and more widely available than on the mainland. In addition, American performers of jazz and classical music regularly attracted larger audiences for concerts in local communities than in auditoriums on the bases.

Fears were occasionally expressed in the Japanese press that this cultural influx would cause Okinawa to become overly Americanized. Novelist Kawabata Yasunari put this false issue in perspective when, after a visit to Okinawa in 1959, he commented that the "Americanization" of Tokyo seemed far more pronounced than anything he had seen in Okinawa.[71] As on the mainland, young people in Okinawa drank soda, wore blue jeans, and listened to rock music. And many studied English conversation, which was taught in several places by American military personnel or their dependents. But an interest in the English language or American arts and culture had not led in Okinawa to the wholesale adoption of American values and lifestyles, as some on the mainland had imagined.

Even popular trends in dress, hairstyles, and hobbies, to the extent that they are of American origin, usually have come to Okinawa indirectly from the mainland and not via Americans stationed on the island. Moreover, the cultural interaction that has taken place runs two ways. U.S. military and civilian personnel have attended local performances of folk music, taken lessons in the martial arts at private Okinawan academies, and studied Japanese language at the Friendship Centers. And despite resentment generated by the thoughtless acts of some Americans, a large number of close professional and personal relationships have developed over the years across the barriers of the bifurcated society.

Still, if U.S. policymakers hoped that subsidized and unsubsidized exposure to American culture would affect political opinions in Okinawa, they were sorely disappointed. A vivid illustration of ambivalent feelings toward the United States could be found during the later 1960s in coffee shops near the University of the Ryu-

---

[71] Kawabata's remarks are cited in E. G. Seidensticker, "The View from Okinawa," *Japan Quarterly* 6:1 (January–March 1959): 38.

kyus, where posters on the walls denounced U.S. involvement in Vietnam while stereos played records of Miles Davis or Chet Atkins. During this turbulent period many students from Okinawa attending universities there and on the mainland declared an affinity with the American antiwar movement.

In more tangible expressions of sentiment through elections and opinion polls, consistent voting for reversion and military reduction culminated in November 1968 with the first popular election of a chief executive for the Government of the Ryukyu Islands. The election of a chief executive, formerly chosen by the G.R.I. legislature subject to the high commissioner's approval, was recommended with misgivings by the then-commissioner Lieutenant General Ferdinand T. Unger. He recalled in 1975 that he "was not unmindful that such a change risked the election of a member of the opposition parties." However, considering the "political uproar" in Okinawa, he expressed the "firm belief that the alternative of denying a popular election of a Chief Executive would certainly bring the functioning of the Government of Ryukyu Islands to a standstill, setting up conditions requiring me to exercise, perhaps, full authority in the archipelago, which in turn could provide an even greater escalation of the reversion movement." General Unger viewed the election as a "palliative [that] might momentarily satisfy Okinawan aspirations and thereby give us more time in putting off the day when our freedom of military operations would be circumscribed."[72]

During the campaign General Unger issued a directive advising U.S. personnel of "the necessity to reduce unfavorable incidents" and "provide better U.S.-Ryukyuan understanding."[73] The U.S. military also gave strong, if unofficial, support to the candidate of Okinawa's conservative party (Okinawa Liberal Democratic Party), Nishime Junji. Despite these efforts and the dire predictions of the conservatives that Nishime's defeat would lead to economic disaster, former schoolteacher Yara Chōbyō, candidate of a coalition of opposition parties, won by a comfortable margin.[74] His platform called not only for immediate reversion and military reduction, but also for an end to U.S. involvement in

---

[72] From General Unger's interview of April 29, 1975, p. 28.

[73] Ibid., p. 19.

[74] Figures from Watanabe, p. 68: Yara Chōbyō (Opposition), 237,562; Nishime Junji (Conservative), 206,011.

Vietnam and the termination of the U.S.-Japan Security Treaty, due for renewal two years later, under which U.S. bases were permitted on the mainland.

The election did not cause fundamental changes in government policies, but it heightened pressures for reversion during negotiations leading up to a meeting between Prime Minister Satō and President Nixon scheduled for the following year. The summit conference in November 1969 produced a communiqué announcing a reversion agreement effective in 1972. Although a major goal had been achieved, the agreement met with widespread dissatisfaction in Okinawa and on the mainland. Of particular concern were vague wordings with regard to the mission and deployment of military forces remaining on the island after reversion. The agreement did not specifically prohibit bringing nuclear weapons there as many hoped it would. Nor did it place any limitations on the dispatching of troops to areas of conflict.[75] Activists in Okinawa and on the mainland organized a series of demonstrations in 1969 and 1970 over the reversion agreement and the security treaty. Public protests subsided after U.S. withdrawal from Vietnam was well under way, however, and the Japanese government arranged for the automatic renewal of the security treaty without Diet debate.

Some thorny problems cropped up when Okinawa rejoined the Japanese political and economic entity in May 1972, although the change was less disruptive than some had predicted. Prices rose sharply with the conversion of dollars to yen, and the rerouting of traffic from right side to left side became a complicated and costly undertaking. The economic benefits of reversion were soon visible with the construction of new department stores, hotels, and office buildings. Predictable strains developed, however, when mainland corporations moved into business sectors previously serviced by local enterprises and purchased large tracts of farmland for private golf courses and vacation lodges. Tourism, more than any other industry, has helped to lead Okinawa's economy away from dependence on military expenditures; but local merchants complained that "Ocean Expo," organized by the Japanese government in 1975 to commemorate reversion and bring in tourist monies, actually cost them more to put on than the income it produced. Clearing the land for Ocean Expo and other tourist facilities is said to have further harmed the natural environment already damaged

---

75 Arasaki, pp. 300–350; and Shinzato, Taminato, and Kinjō, pp. 243–244.

by the bases. And recently, scientists have discovered that the enormous proliferation of construction projects throughout the island has caused a serious erosion of topsoil, destroying the coral that gives Okinawa's landscape much of the breathtaking beauty that attracts tourists.

A coherent development policy is essential to protect the environment and continue advancing the standard of living, which has risen significantly since 1972.[76] The growing economy is evident not only in the construction boom that has transformed Naha and the city of Nago to the north, but in the increasing number of luxury consumer goods in the stores and late-model cars on the roads. As part of its 2.4-trillion-yen investment between 1972 and 1987 to improve the local infrastructure, the Japanese government has financed a network of neatly paved highways, banked by attractive landscaping, that reaches even into remote rural areas previously served only by dirt roads. Monies from the national treasury have also been used to erect or refurbish public buildings and schools, including a new and vastly larger campus for the University of the Ryukyus, built originally by the United States in 1950, which now rivals in space and facilities a number of prestigious universities on the mainland. These highly visible projects and rising per capita income are often cited to explain the trend among voters in the 1980s to choose local candidates of the ruling conservative party in prefecture-wide elections. Nevertheless, opposition parties regained the governorship in the 1990s in large part because the conservatives had failed to negotiate significant reductions in the military bases.

Support for opposition parties and continuing protest demonstrations reflect the deep concern in Okinawa about what did not change after reversion. More than two decades later the number of U.S troops and square miles occupied by bases still represent about three-quarters of the U.S. military presence in all of Japan.[77] While a few parcels of U.S. government property have been

---

[76] Although the per capita income of local residents rose from 60 percent of the national average at the time of reversion to 74 percent in 1987, it is still the lowest of all prefectures, and unemployment is twice the national average. From lead editorial in *Asahi Shinbun*, May 15, 1987.

[77] General Unger reported that in November 1968 there were 43,000 American forces in Okinawa (interview of April 29, 1975, p. 18). Figures supplied by the Department of Defense indicated that about 30,000 of the 45,000 U.S. troops stationed in all of Japan during 1995 were stationed in Okinawa. Okinawa represents approximately one percent of Japan's population and land area.

turned over to local authorities, a number of bases have been transferred in whole or in part to Japan's Self-Defense Forces (SDF) despite the continuing shortage of land for civilian use. People complain that, on these bases, all that has changed is "the color of the uniforms" as military objectives continue to take precedence over the interests of local residents. Feeling against the growing number of Self-Defense Forces has been particularly intense, owing both to resentment over the problems associated with their presence and to memories of atrocities committed by Japanese soldiers against civilians in Okinawa during World War II. Protests have disrupted military parades, and some restaurant owners and innkeepers have refused to serve SDF personnel.

The focus of concern over the American military presence has shifted somewhat since reversion. The number of crimes committed annually by U.S. forces and their dependents against local residents is about one-fifth what it was in the mid-1960s.[78] Robbery, assault, and disorderly conduct are down sharply, although traffic accidents involving U.S. personnel, including a number caused by drunk driving, continue to take their toll. Observers attribute this welcome reduction in part to a greater awareness among young Americans of being in a foreign country where they are subject to local laws and to arrest by the police if they get into trouble. American commanders receive special briefings emphasizing that the U.S. military will remain in Okinawa only with the permission of the Japanese government, and they are directed to inculcate sensitivity toward the local community among their troops.[79] But perhaps the largest factor in the decline of GI crime is economic. With the improvement of the economy and the revaluation of the yen, most Americans cannot easily afford to amuse themselves in bars, more of which now cater to local clientele or visitors from the mainland. Military personnel have turned increasingly to service clubs on the bases for their leisure activities. This trend, along with official "clean-up" efforts, has led to the shrinking or disappearance of some of the more notorious

---

[78] Crime figures between 1972 and 1983 are 219 in 1972, 310 in 1973, 318 in 1974, 223 in 1975, 263 in 1976, 342 in 1977, 288 in 1978, 274 in 1979, 321 in 1980, 253 in 1981, 234 in 1982, and 195 in 1983. Cited in *Okinawa no kichi* (Bases in Okinawa) (Naha: Okinawa Taimusu Sha, 1984). Compare with prereversion figures in n. 40.

[79] Interviews in July 1987 with Mrs. Chisato Fanner, Office of Community Relations, U.S. Army in Okinawa, and Colonel James H. Griffin, commander of all U.S. Army forces in Okinawa.

"amusement areas," although GI bars and hotels still occupy several blocks in towns near the larger American bases.

While off-duty crime and misbehavior of U.S. forces remain a problem, people in Okinawa seem more troubled today by dangers and disruptions resulting from activities carried out by military personnel as part of their official mission. Political pressures, backed by protest demonstrations, intensify both when large-scale exercises cause increased noise, congestion, and accidents and when the United States proposes to build facilities or undertake new activities that threaten the quality of life in a particular area.[80] The enormous military presence keeps the island a center of attention for antiwar groups in Japan and elsewhere, some of which organized a peace demonstration that drew approximately 18,000 participants to Kadena Air Base on June 21, 1987, despite a steady rain throughout the day. And, as if to illustrate the continuing irony of Okinawa's economic link to the U.S. military, the base employees' labor union staged a demonstration two weeks later to protest layoffs of local workers at American service clubs.

Although protests continue in front of U.S. bases, people in Okinawa voice their grievances more often today at the various prefectural offices of the Japanese government, which now has the ultimate authority over matters military and civilian. Rejoining the Japanese political entity has given people access, through their elected representatives, to those in Tokyo whose decisions affect their lives. Yet there is a widespread feeling among local residents that, after Okinawa faded from the headlines in the early 1970s, people in other parts of Japan became insensitive to the island's continuing problems. This feeling, and some heavy-handed efforts by the Japanese Ministry of Education to promote patriotism in the local schools, have given added impetus in recent years to an ardent regionalism. People in Okinawa have always been proud of their culture and history, but while before reversion they often spoke to outside visitors of their affinity with other Japanese, they now seem more inclined to emphasize aspects

---

[80] In two recent cases, the building of a helicopter pad near Ginoza village led to bitter protests as did the proposed addition of a flight training facility to a marine installation near Aha village in northern Okinawa. People in and around Aha pointed out that noise of the aircraft would disrupt their lives and destroy the tranquility of one of the most beautiful rural landscapes on the island. (Interview in July 1987 with Mr. Uehara Yasunari, Kunigami village councilman.)

of their culture and outlook that distinguish them from people elsewhere in Japan. For their part, visitors from the mainland arrive to comfortable accommodations and beautiful surroundings, but many seem to remain in strangely isolated clusters as they wend their way on shopping tours through department stores or file off buses behind flag-carrying guides at World War II battle sites. Reversion was a cause for celebration, but to local residents, many of those who travel nowadays from the mainland (freely and without passports) to swim in the ocean, tour the war memorials, and buy souvenirs seem all but oblivious to what people in Okinawa have endured past and present.

Cocktail Party

Ōshiro Tatsuhiro

Cocktail Party

Ōshiro Tatsuhiro

PRELUDE

I gave Mr. Miller's name and house number to the guard. After telephoning to make sure I was expected, he showed me the route from the guard shack to the house.

"Is it really all right for me to go in like this?" I asked.

"Yes, you won't have any trouble." The guard answered expressionlessly, as if he found nothing peculiar about my question. He seemed inured to the monotony of his routine. The road through the security gate split into two neatly paved streets which ran far back among the long rows of houses. Deep in their midst, the streets divided again and again into a labyrinth of interconnecting branches. This section of a vast American army post is known officially as Base Housing, but Okinawans call it "the family brigade."

Its maze of twisting streets had been the scene of a frightening experience for me ten years before. That afternoon had also been hot and muggy, but unlike today I had come to do an errand in the town near the base, not to visit someone I knew inside. On my way home I was seized with a sudden impulse. By chance the guard was away from his shack, though this seems now like an unfortunate coincidence. In that moment I decided to try crossing through the family brigade as a shortcut to the east. I was sure I could reach the local branch of a bank on the other side of this wide stretch of land. Exploring unfamiliar roads had fascinated me since childhood.

Yielding to my curiosity, I slipped past the guard shack and started walking. However, after about twenty minutes, I knew I had miscalculated. I thought it would take fifteen minutes to walk straight through the base, or not more than twenty if I strolled along leisurely sightseeing. But even after half an hour, I still couldn't see anything that vaguely resembled the wire fence at the east end. All the houses looked exactly alike. Only the shapes of the shrubbery varied occasionally. But by the color and pattern of laundry hanging in the yards, I could see that I was walking in circles, around and around on the same street.

None of the foreigners or Okinawan maids I passed seemed to notice that I was a stranger. But when I realized I was lost, panic seized me. In my mind I tried desperately to cling to the notion that the housing area was, after all, inside the very same township where I lived, but it was no use. Struggling to maintain my composure, I stopped one of the maids and asked her how to get to the east end. She showed me the way impassively. Her placid, self-possessed air gave the impression she was someone who belonged here and made me feel a vast distance between us.

At last I managed to find my way to the rear exit at the east end. When I got home and told my wife what had happened, she was shocked that I had entered the base, recalling her own experience working for a laundry chain that serviced the military.

"The man in our store who had to make deliveries there was mistaken for a thief and turned over to the MPs. So, you see, it can happen even if you carry a pass."

Now, ten years later, I still couldn't enjoy walking alone as much as I had before, and felt especially wary around the base. I would be less concerned if I were still a bachelor, but my wife keeps reminding me of my family obligations. I suppose a father can never be too careful.

Before the war, people could travel easily to any remote corner of Okinawa, but those times have long passed. I wondered about the maids who worked in the housing area. Perhaps the guards, because they carried rifles, were not afraid. There were occasional newspaper reports of foreign children throwing stones or shooting BB guns at the windows of local buses. Surely those children weren't afraid walking the streets unarmed among the Okinawans. Or were they? And what about Robert Harris, the soldier who rented our rear apartment to share with his girlfriend? Though he stayed there only two or three days a week, I wondered if he ever felt apprehensive in a town inhabited entirely by Okinawans.

But today I felt good. After all, I'd been invited to Mr. Miller's party. So if I were stopped, all I'd have to do was give his name, house number, and phone number, and everything would be all right.

Mr. Miller could be so charming. He had dropped in at my office one day to invite me. *"Chi wei chiu hui,"* he'd said in Chinese. I understood *chiu hui,* a liquor party, but couldn't imagine what he meant by *chi wei,* which is a chicken's tail. A few days later I received his invitation card with a picture of a rooster and the English word "cocktail." Then I realized that what he'd said to me in Chinese was a literal translation of "cocktail party." It amused me that by chance I had learned some Chinese from an American.

"I've invited Mr. Sun, Mr. Ogawa, and some of my other friends. Altogether, there should be fourteen or fifteen of us," Mr. Miller had told me. Mr. Sun is a Chinese lawyer practicing in Okinawa, Mr. Ogawa a newspaper reporter from mainland Japan. The four of us had formed what we called a "Chinese language research group," though we met only to practice speaking Chinese. We made every effort to avoid using English, though sometimes I wondered why we spoke only Chinese, since English practice would have been good for Mr. Sun, Mr. Ogawa, and me. Perhaps it was because we had started meeting at Mr. Miller's invitation. It didn't seem to matter, though. The important thing was that we'd been able to form a Chinese conversation group in this place where almost everyone is either Japanese or American. This is what held together our special friendship. Once a month we met at a club on the base where a table was reserved in Mr. Miller's name.

I hadn't heard whether any of the other guests invited to the party tonight were interested in speaking Chinese, but this didn't matter much to me either. We'd been introduced once to Mrs. Miller at the club, and my first thought now was that I could have another look at her beautiful face and voluptuous figure. And, of course, we'd be able to enjoy the fine liquor none of us local people could ever afford on our salaries. Almost before I realized it, I had begun to take pleasure in things that had nothing to do with our Chinese conversation fellowship. Not the least of these was the military club where we gathered every month. Meals there were tax free, so we could eat and drink quite cheaply. It was also a place to which only a few local people were admitted. My pleasure was somehow enhanced by the feeling that I'd been chosen to enjoy these privileges.

Forgetting the muggy heat, I was in high spirits now as I passed among the houses in the family brigade.

I arrived to find most of the guests already assembled.

"Latecomers chug three drinks to catch up." Speaking in Japanese, Mr. Ogawa gave me the familiar greeting for late arrivals at parties. This young reporter for a first-rate newspaper then asked me to translate what he had just said into Chinese.

"Hou lai tso shang." I lifted my glass in a toast as I responded with "latecomers drink in the 'seat of honor.'"

"That's wrong," he said. "It means 'the late bird takes the lead.'"

"No, that's the standard translation in Japan," I countered. "But I don't think it comes as close to the original Chinese."

"Tsen mo liao?" Mr. Sun asked what we were arguing about as he came over to join us. He smiled and lifted his glass, which was still nearly full of a reddish sloe gin brewed to women's tastes. It was obvious that, for a Chinese, this highly skilled lawyer wasn't much of a drinker.

"How do you say *hou lai tso shang* in English?" I asked. Since Mr. Sun couldn't speak Japanese, there was no other way to settle the question.

"In English?" Mr. Sun's thin eyebrows shot up suddenly on his wide forehead. "But there is no seat of honor at parties in the West."

It was impossible to tell if Mr. Sun was trying to be funny or to hide the fact that he couldn't answer the question. In any case, his reply had us both laughing.

"You folks enjoying yourselves?" someone asked in English. A foreigner about my height approached us. His Ronald Coleman–style mustache suited him well. Mr. Miller came over quickly to introduce us.

"This is Mr. Morgan from next door. He's an engineer with the Army Maintenance Department."

"Why didn't you say that in Chinese?" Mr. Morgan teased. Mr. Miller, much the taller of the two, hovered over Mr. Morgan as though he were peering straight down at that Ronald Coleman mustache.

"So you'd know I wasn't slipping any secrets into your introduction."

"Glad to meet you," I said. "Mr. Miller has told us about you."

Mr. Morgan lifted his drink in a toast. Just as he and I clinked our glasses, Mrs. Miller carried in the food.

"Turkey, anyone?"

From the plunging neckline of a black one-piece dress, her

white breasts billowed up full. The sight was dazzling. I was busily loading my plate with food when Mr. Morgan spoke again.

"Your forming a Chinese conversation group in Okinawa makes a lot of sense historically, you know." A note of affectation had crept into his voice, and I suspected that Mr. Morgan shared a misconception widely held by Americans and mainland Japanese who thought Okinawa was a dominion of China before 1868. I quickly reached for my food and took a big mouthful of turkey. When I looked up, Mr. Morgan had gone over to Mr. Ogawa and was questioning him vigorously.

"Speaking as a reporter, do you think it's inevitable that Okinawa will revert to Japanese sovereignty?"

"I don't know if it's inevitable, but I think it's necessary." Mr. Ogawa seemed quite unperturbed, as if he had answered this question many times before.

"Why?"

"Because it shouldn't remain under the present occupation rule."

"I agree," Mr. Morgan nodded. "But why can't Okinawa consider becoming independent? I've read that it was an independent country until the nineteenth century."

Mr. Ogawa smiled. Then, excusing himself, he went over to the bar to refill his drink.

"Of course, you two have read about the nineteenth century, haven't you?" Mr. Morgan peered inquisitively over his Ronald Coleman mustache, first at Mr. Sun, then at me. He continued without waiting for Mr. Ogawa to return. "Well, I can cite evidence that the concept of Okinawan independence is still viable today. Have you read *Okinawa: The History of an Island People,* by George Kerr?"

This Mr. Morgan is a real chatterbox, I thought. Like other Americans, he had obviously learned from Kerr's book about the Shimazu daimyo's exploitation of the Ryūkyū Islands after invading them in the seventeenth century and about the Japanese government's discriminatory treatment of Okinawa after it became a prefecture in 1879. Kerr's book had become the source for virtually everything written about Okinawan history by American officials.

"That book was...," I hesitated. Somehow I couldn't bring myself to say it was written to justify U.S. foreign policy. "That book influences so many Americans' views on Okinawa," I answered instead.

"Are you saying it's wrong?" Mr. Morgan looked surprised.

Standing nearby, Ogawa sipped his refilled drink and watched me with a wide grin on his face.

"Your question reminds me of something a Chinese army officer asked me just after the war." I decided to try another tack. "The Japanese military had assigned me as an interpreter on the outskirts of Shanghai. The Chinese officers I worked with were very kind, and we all got on well together. One of them said to me, 'You're Ryukyuan and therefore one of us. Why are you working for the Japanese military?'"

Mr. Morgan's mustache bobbed up and down as he nodded vehemently, though I wasn't sure why. Now he and Mr. Miller, smiling broadly, both turned to look at Mr. Sun. Mr. Sun stared back at me with a kind of half-smile.

"I told the officer he was tempted to ask such a question because, in China, the Ryukyus are thought to be a Chinese domain from ancient times. But we are taught that they were originally part of Japan. So, you see, everyone's view depends on how he was educated. Only God knows the truth."

"You're too clever for me." Mr. Morgan laughed, opening his mouth very wide. "It must be the wisdom you've gained from Okinawa's long history."

Now I laughed, too. Then, having no desire to continue this discussion, I looked down at my plate of food and began stuffing my mouth with ham, vegetable salad, and boiled egg. Mr. Morgan also seemed satisfied to leave it at that, and, jiggling his drink, he moved away.

"Are your children well?" Mr. Miller asked in Chinese. His tone suggested that he wanted to shift the conversation to a gentler topic.

"I have only one daughter," I said. My daughter was a high school student who attended a private English conversation school at night where Mrs. Miller was an instructor. This had also brought our two families together.

"Oh, that's right. But it's too bad, isn't it? One child isn't really enough." Mr. Miller made a serious face. "We have three now and wish we had more."

"Do you mind if I check that with your wife?"

"Go ahead. She asked all her students about their families and found that we now have the average number of children. But she still wants more."

"What is the ideal number of children supposed to be in America?"

"Don't lots of them make a happier family?"

"Maybe, as long as they can be raised successfully."

"Oh, come now. People in Okinawa are always complaining about how hard it is to make a living," Mr. Miller said, then turned toward Mr. Ogawa. "Wasn't it once the custom in your part of Japan to abandon old people in the mountains when supporting them became too much of a burden?"

"There are many legends about that. I believe it was practiced throughout most of the country at one time or another, though not particularly in my prefecture." After his purposely ambiguous reply, Mr. Ogawa turned to me. "Didn't this also happen in Okinawa?"

"I haven't heard of it, but there does seem to have been a brutal custom called 'thinning out' for ending the lives of newborns."

"Yes, I believe that was the regent Sai On's policy in the eighteenth century." Mr. Ogawa took this opportunity to display his erudition. "According to what I've read, ancient rulers were deeply troubled over the population problem, though if such cruel measures were accepted, they can't really be said to have agonized all that much."

What Mr. Ogawa said reminded me that overpopulation still poses a critical dilemma in the twentieth century. Some people even claim that war is mankind's way of dealing with it. The image of atomic bombs instantly reducing the world's population flashed through my mind, and I wondered if Mr. Ogawa or Mr. Miller might be thinking along the same lines. Having no desire to confirm my suspicions, I turned to Mr. Sun.

"Were such things practiced in China, too?"

"I'm no expert on history or legends, but in three thousand years I suppose the Chinese must have gone through every conceivable ordeal at one time or another."

Mr. Sun peered out at me gently from behind thick glasses set below his wide forehead, and I remembered that he was one of the people who had left for Hong Kong when the Chinese Communists took control of the mainland. He had told me once that, after seeing Chinese Communist soldiers kill two of his three children, he had fled, leaving his wife and last remaining child behind. To this day he had heard nothing from them. I'd wanted to ask him more about his life in China because, like me, he had lived in Shanghai. But he never talked about it, and I sensed in his reluctance the magnitude of his suffering during his last years there.

"I remember reading in Kuo Mo-jo's novel *Waves* about World War II in China." Mr. Ogawa spoke with journalistic matter-of-factness. "Isn't there a scene of a mother who chokes her screaming child to death when she hears the roar of approaching Japanese warplanes?"

Mr. Sun nodded slowly, his face expressionless. He seemed hard-pressed to keep up his end of the conversation.

"This happened in Okinawa too," I began, turning to face Mr. Ogawa. "In fact...," and again I hesitated. I wanted to tell him that on occasion Japanese soldiers had killed children. "Oh, let's drop it," I said instead. "No more talk of war while we're drinking." Yet I had the feeling we were really talking about something beyond war itself, though at this point I had no desire to pursue the matter.

"By the way," piped up Mr. Miller, "the writer you just mentioned. Is he in Taiwan or Hong Kong?"

"Neither," Mr. Ogawa answered nonchalantly. "Kuo Mo-jo lives in Peking. And he holds an important government post there, doesn't he?" Ogawa now turned to look at Mr. Sun, who forced a wry smile in apparent agreement.

"Peking?" Mr. Miller tried to hide his obvious discomfort by taking a furtive sip of his drink.

"Mr. Miller, you should at least acknowledge the name of a major novelist." From Ogawa's voice it was clear that his steady consumption of liquor was beginning to have its effect. "You Americans would assume that a Chinese Communist writer is automatically a traitor, an enemy of all mankind...," Ogawa interrupted himself with a hasty apology. "Well, you might not go quite that far. Still, America's attitude of total aloofness toward mainland China can cause your country nothing but trouble."

I waited nervously to see how Mr. Miller would reply, expecting him to try a bit of forced humor to head off an argument, but he maintained his familiar smile.

"Does Okinawa have a native literature?" Mr. Sun asked, turning to me.

"Do you mean native in form? In subject matter?"

"Well, now that you ask, I'm not really sure." Mr. Sun broke into his first smile in some time. "I guess I mean a literature distinct from Japan's."

"The Okinawa dialect is actually a form of Japanese," I began. "Oh, by the way, please forget what I said before about education being the source of everyone's opinions." I was determined to keep the discussion pleasant. "Literature in Okinawa dates from the thirteenth century and continues to be written today, but since it has always been composed in Japanese it would be difficult to call it distinct from Japan's."

"Of course Okinawa has a native literature," Ogawa cut in. "Surely your marvelous classical dance and poetry are distinct."

"I don't think so."

"Just because the language is a form of Japanese? That's ridiculous. Culture should never be viewed so narrowly. Okinawans are clearly Japanese, in spite of what Mr. Sun and other Chinese might think, but any outsider can see that your culture is unique."

"That word 'unique' bothers me. People from the mainland call Okinawan culture unique to separate it from their own. But why not think of it as a local variety of Japanese culture?"

"Oh, come now. Okinawans invented the word 'mainland.' You put yourselves in a separate category, so how can you deny your culture is unique?"

"Just a moment. Somehow we seem to have gotten into a two-way conversation in Japanese," I said. "This must be terribly boring for Mr. Sun."

"You were the one who started speaking Japanese," Ogawa retorted.

Now, hearing his name, Mr. Sun seemed to catch the latest drift of our conversation and began laughing. Soon the others joined in. Just then Mrs. Miller came over to pass around the food. Mr. Ogawa lost no time drawing her into the debate.

"Ma'am, what do you think of Okinawa's unique culture?" he asked in English.

"Oh, it's wonderful!" Mrs. Miller answered promptly. "I just love their pottery and the way they dye cloth here. And the traditional music and dance—they're all just wonderful!"

"Do you think it's part of Japanese culture, or something separate?"

"Basically they're the same, aren't they? But it does have a certain individuality...No, maybe that's wrong. Basically it's different, but rather close to Japanese culture."

"Which is it then?"

"I really don't know." Shrugging her fully rounded shoulders, she laughed loudly. "I'm the hostess here, so I'd better go serve this food." My eyes followed her voluptuous figure as she laughed again and moved away.

"That reminds me," said Mr. Ogawa, "of what a Japanese writer said about Okinawan food when he came here a few years ago. He called it pallid. Isn't it strange that a culture producing richly colored dyes and pottery should have such plain-looking food?"

"Maybe it's meant to symbolize hardship," said Mr. Miller. "I know very little about Okinawan food, but from the one or two times I tried it, I'd say it was close to Chinese food."

"Is that supposed to prove that Okinawa's culture has its origins in China?" Ogawa cut in.

"No, you're getting ahead of me," Mr. Miller laughed. "I'm only saying the food looks plain. But isn't it true, Mr. Sun, that Chinese food was created by people who struggled with poverty over the centuries?"

"That's what we're taught," said Mr. Sun cautiously. "China's three-thousand-year history of famines and wars is said to have produced a nourishing cuisine, the art of making food from whatever nature provides when times are hard."

"You never know what good will come from misfortune!" Mr. Ogawa spoke with an exaggerated look of wonder and admiration on his face. Then he suddenly turned to me. "People in Okinawa could create something, too, if they put their minds to it. So they can cope with their present situation."

"You mean because we're not ready for reversion to Japan yet?"

"No, and please don't put words in my mouth. I only meant that reversion is not likely to come soon, but you must not give up the struggle."

"So what should we create?"

"Nourishment for the spirit that will sustain you no matter how bad things get."

What Mr. Ogawa said made me wonder if he might be a member of the *burakumin* minority that has suffered discrimination in Japan since medieval times. I had once assumed only Okinawan intellectuals so thoroughly romanticized stoicism, but later it occurred to me that perhaps the *burakumin* on the mainland did, too. And what about the Chinese, I wondered now, and turned again to Mr. Sun.

"The Chinese have a special talent for learning foreign languages, don't they?"

"Yes, I suppose you're right."

"Don't be so quick to agree with me." I laughed uncomfortably as I tried to explain. "When I was at the academy in Shanghai, I was always amazed at how well the townspeople could speak Japanese."

"It was the only way they could make a living under Japanese occupation," said Mr. Sun.

"Yes, I suppose it was a skill born of necessity. I heard people there used English a lot before the Japanese invasion, and again after the war." At this point I barely avoided repeating an insulting "joke" I had heard from a Japanese classmate in Shanghai: People of a ruined nation learn languages instinctively. "It makes me wonder why Okinawans aren't better at English nowadays," I said instead.

"But they're all quite good, aren't they?"

"No. A few speak it well, but the general level is low, especially comparing, for example, our students with those in Japan." Unable to think of a suitable Chinese word for "Japanese mainland," I realized now that I had fallen into the habit of calling it "Japan."

"That's so true," Mr. Ogawa butted in again. "Though with all the Americans here, Okinawans certainly have more chances to practice. Maybe they don't work hard enough at it."

"We should ask Mrs. Miller," said Mr. Sun. "She's had lots of experience teaching English to Okinawans."

There was a rare hint of playfulness in his suggestion. Unfortunately, Mrs. Miller was busy with some foreigners on the other side of the room.

"The trouble people have learning English here is closely related to their problems with standard Japanese," I said, expressing an opinion I'd held for some time. "They are seriously handicapped from the beginning by the geographic and linguistic separation."

"Aha! So now you admit the cultures are separate," Ogawa said sarcastically, and I realized I had just demolished my own argument that Okinawan culture should be considered a part of Japan's.

"Well, no...I mean...uh...that is..." Unable to counter him, I succeeded in making a joke of my obvious predicament, and soon the others were laughing again.

"Speaking of language," said Mr. Sun, "I understand a lot of Okinawa dialect is derived from Chinese."

"I would expect to hear that from you," I said with another laugh. "It reminds me of when I first entered the academy in

Shanghai and my classmates told me I should be good in Chinese as they assumed all students from Okinawa were."

"No, no! That's not what I meant." Mr. Sun waved his hands in frustration. "I'm only making a simple observation, not like those Chinese officers who helped you discover your eminent theory of education." He laughed nervously as he tried to explain. "I was just remembering that an elderly intellectual here told me that many words of Okinawa dialect have Chinese origins."

"Oh? What are they?" Mr. Miller leaned toward us with heightened interest.

"Well, I heard that *tārī* meaning 'father' comes from *ta ren* in Chinese.

"That's right," I said. "It was a word used in families of Okinawa's samurai elite. *Jīfā*, meaning 'hairpin,' comes from *chieh fa*. And the *tung tao p'en* trays for serving food on special occasions in China are called *tondā bon* here." I rattled off five or six more examples, then continued. "In a village about seven miles from here, traditional *tāfākū* dances are still performed. The titles of the accompanying songs have survived, though the texts have not. I was asked about them, but have no idea what the words might have been."

"Someone once taught me the words to the *Haryū* boat race song," he said. "It's quite a beautiful poem."

"That reminds me of the *Pēron* racing boats in Nagasaki." Mr. Ogawa took over. "They also originated in China. Where was it anyway? Not Shanghai or Fuchow."

Pondering this question, Ogawa stared straight ahead as though lost deep in thought. His eyebrows, wrinkled from drinking, gave his face a strangely comical expression. As I watched him, Mr. Morgan came into view, glanced over at us for a moment, then hurried to the front door and went out.

"The *Pēron* and *Haryū* boats. What a strange coincidence!" Ogawa seemed to have abandoned his search for their origin. "Were they brought from the Ryukyus to Nagasaki, or from Nagasaki to the Ryukyus?"

"They might have reached both places from the same source," I chimed in.

"Maybe so. Japanese pirates could have brought them over about the sixteenth century."

"That's impossible. Pirates don't transport such things."

"I suppose not. But you have to admit it's nice to think so." After apologizing to Mr. Sun for slipping again into Japanese,

Ogawa began a lecture on Japanese pirates. "They raided China, Okinawa, and Japan as well, Mr. Sun, so you see they didn't discriminate against any people in particular. And besides, they served the cause of cultural exchange."

"That's a dangerous assumption. Aren't you glorifying aggression?" Mr. Sun interjected quickly, and I was reminded that Americans had brought various aspects of their culture to Okinawa. I turned to look at Mr. Miller, but he had disappeared from our midst. The noisy babble of the other guests was beginning to get on my nerves.

"I don't mean to glorify aggression, Mr. Sun, but you have to look at history with a long view. Then you can see how the cultures of various nations expand and interact. If I may digress for a moment, I think we should view China's historical connection to Nagasaki and Okinawa as a kind of romantic destiny."

"I can't accept that." Mr. Sun spoke calmly, but with a note of persistence in his voice that startled me. "No matter how much you may want to see it as serving culture, aggression is still aggression and *not* a service. That's what the long view of history teaches us."

For Mr. Sun, who never seemed to challenge anything directly, it was a rare, slashing rebuttal. Ogawa stared at Mr. Sun in amazement and looked as if he had sobered up all at once. His expression made me want to laugh. At the same time, I sensed Mr. Sun had revealed a deeply held conviction, and I wanted to draw him out further. Then, taking another look around me, I restrained both urges and lifted my glass to my mouth instead. At that moment Mr. Miller called everyone to silence.

"It's a shame to interrupt all this merrymaking, but could we stop for a while to lend Mr. Morgan a hand? His three-year-old son didn't come home for supper tonight and still hasn't turned up. He's called everyone in the neighborhood, but no one has seen the boy. Mr. Morgan was unaware of this and was enjoying himself here with the rest of us, but now..."

"We must help him all we can," added a man I judged to be the youngest of the guests. He looked as if he might be of Mexican descent, and impressed me as especially kind.

* * *

We went outside to begin searching. As I walked through the family brigade, the vague anxiety I'd felt losing my way here ten years before came back to me. I tried to describe my feelings to Mr. Sun who for some reason was walking close beside me.

"The whole area is so bare—nothing but houses and open fields. That's what worries me. There's no way a child could have hidden, no place to hide."

"Well, we can try looking around anyway," he said.

I agreed, telling myself I had no reason to panic as I had a decade ago. I knew the number of Mr. Miller's house and would not be likely to lose my way this time. Walking along with Mr. Sun, I felt somewhat reassured, as if I were carrying papers that would identify me to anyone who might stop us.

Countless stars sparkled overhead. But the warm air was heavy with humidity, and I wondered if a typhoon might be brewing somewhere to the south. The wind high above us seemed to be stirring restlessly; and the stars, lacking their usual tranquility, flickered in fitful patterns.

"People say Okinawa's night sky is beautiful. How about China's?" I asked casually, having quite forgotten the anxiety that must have weighed heavily on Mr. Morgan. We had slowed to a leisurely pace, as if we were merely out for a walk.

"You've been to China too," said Mr. Sun.

"Yes, but I've already forgotten what it was like." In fact, the scenery south of the Yangtze River had faded almost entirely from my memory after twenty years.

"You should always have beautiful memories of your homeland, I suppose. Unfortunately, I drifted from Shanghai, where I was born, to Nanking, Hunan, Kiangsi, and Kwangsi, so now my impressions of these places are all jumbled up in my mind."

I knew that what Mr. Sun called his "drifting" was actually a migration forced on him by the advancing Japanese army. The truth was that moving constantly from one place to another had left no room in his memory for scenic impressions.

"Even so...," I began, but quickly changed the subject. "There's no excuse for our loafing like this. What should we do?"

"The others seem to have turned down another street, so let's try asking at each of the houses along here."

I agreed to his suggestion, but for a moment I again felt the apprehension of ten years before. Here we were, an Okinawan and a Chinese, knocking on these Americans' doors in the middle of the night. Of course, our visits would be justified once we explained that we were looking for a lost American child. Still, it wasn't going to be easy. In the first place, I wondered how we would handle the extremely troublesome procedure of continually introducing ourselves.

"Let's go as friends of Mr. Morgan," suggested Mr. Sun with a smile.

"Of course," I thought and forced a smile of my own.

As it turned out, we had no trouble. To my relief, as soon as we said we were friends of Mr. Morgan, everyone understood why we had come. People told us they had received a phone call, and though no one knew where the child might be, they were all very kind. A few of the wives asked if we were both Okinawans, and when Mr. Sun answered that he was Chinese, they reacted with surprise and courtesy.

"I never expected everyone to be so kind," I said. "Living isolated like this in a foreign country probably brings them together, especially when there's trouble."

"That must be it," Mr. Sun said, then paused momentarily before continuing. "And they're all aware of the worst possibility—that he might have been kidnaped."

"Kidnaped? By an Okinawan?"

"No, not necessarily. There are criminals among the foreigners here, too."

His words seemed meant to soothe me, but I still couldn't shake off my own preoccupations. The truth was that my selfish attitude was inexcusable. Perhaps kidnaping had never occurred to me because I cared only superficially about the child's disappearance. Though I had come out to help in the search, seeing the warm sympathy of the Americans we were visiting made me aware of how lacking my own concern was. I'd been far more worried about maintaining my composure inside the family brigade than finding Mr. Morgan's boy.

"This reminds me of something that happened twenty years ago," began Mr. Sun as we came to the fence at the edge of the base. We gazed through the wire mesh, more than three meters high, at the glowing lights of the city beyond. The long lines of oval lamps, which marked the rapid growth of the city in recent years, appeared now like rows of silent faces looking toward us with indifference.

"I'd taken my family as far as the town of W., one stop before Chungking," Mr. Sun continued. "We had two sons then, aged four and two. Our third child hadn't been born yet. The Nationalist government had already moved to Chungking, and most people in the group called 'anti-Japanese patriots' were starting new lives there. But my wife got sick and we couldn't travel to Chungking with the others. After that, I learned all too well how precarious life can be for a family left behind by a government in retreat. Of course, one should never have to depend on any government, but for us it wasn't only that we were abandoned by the Nationalists. The enemy Japanese army caught up with us, and we were forced to live at W. under military occupation. I managed to finagle a 'good citizen's pass' and planned to wait for a chance to escape. However, time passed and I still couldn't get us out of there.

"One day, while we were delayed at W., my eldest son got lost. He had gone out to play with some other children in the neighborhood, but didn't come home that evening. It was wartime, so the streets were pitch dark when I went out to look for him. I was a stranger with few acquaintances in town, and as I walked around visiting people at random, I had this fear that one of them might be a spy who would turn me in. And I could tell that the people I was visiting were worried that I might do the same thing to them. Searching for my son, I had to contend with the mutual distrust and suspicion that plague people who live in the midst of an enemy. I finally heard that he was being held in protective custody at Japanese military police headquarters. But before they would turn him over to me, I was interrogated at length. Somehow I managed to muddle through the questioning. Later, as I walked home through those streets, I wondered if this were really my country and if the people who lived in those long rows of houses could be my countrymen."

I understood why Mr. Sun had remembered this incident. The events he described had much in common with our situation. Yet the problems we faced looking for Mr. Morgan's boy were entirely different. Most important, he was not the son of a family carrying a phony "good citizen's pass" but a child of one of the occupation personnel. The Japanese military police claimed to be holding Mr. Sun's boy in protective custody, though they might actually have kidnaped him for one reason or another. But if an Okinawan had kidnaped the Morgans' boy, what possibly could be his motive? What would lead an Okinawan man or woman to seize the young son of one of the island's occupiers?

Mr. Sun and I stood together in silence.

"Oh, there you are," someone called out unexpectedly. It was the kind-looking young man whom I had thought to be of Mexican descent. "We found the boy. The maid took him home with her on her day off without telling anybody. There's nothing to worry about." He laughed reassuringly.

"That was *some* kidnaping," said Mr. Sun, and we both laughed loudly. Although I had never met the Morgans' maid, it angered me that even a young girl would so thoughtlessly take their son back to her village without permission. At the same time, I was so relieved she had only meant well that I wanted to sing out in celebration.

"Now we know an Okinawan would never kidnap an American child," I said to Mr. Sun.

"It seems inconceivable, doesn't it." He and I exchanged broad smiles as we retraced our steps to Mr. Miller's house.

When we arrived the party had already started again, and the unfortunate incident seemed to be the topic of all conversation. Among the clusters of guests, many people offered opinions about the Morgans' teen-age maid. Inevitably, there was one man who strongly condemned her; but when someone pointed out that her intentions had been good, even he finally agreed. Although I had previously stuck with Miller, Ogawa, and Sun in our little four-man group, for some reason I now hurried around to talk with other foreigners. Everyone seemed determined to make the party's revival as lively as possible.

"You must have been relieved," said the kind-looking young man who had found us standing at the fence. He introduced himself as "Lincoln" and told us he worked at the base theater, where he was in charge of the stage lights. Then he gave a lengthy explanation of how his mother was Mexican and the name "Lincoln" seemed fitting for a child born of international friendship. He was, as I had suspected, a bit of a chatterbox. "It must be awful," he continued, "when guests from abroad lose a child in your country."

I smiled and nodded. There was something troubling about that word "guests," but I assumed Lincoln was only trying to be friendly. We were interrupted by another American who introduced himself as Mr. Fink, the manager of a local car-importing company.

"Now that it's all over, I really can't imagine an Okinawan involved in a crime against an American child," he said. "We had a labor dispute at our company and the union organizers were so anxious to maintain good relations they seemed almost too accommodating."

This was apparently his attempt at flattery, but I didn't mind since he, too, was obviously trying to express his relief in a friendly way.

"He's right, you know," Mr. Ogawa whispered to me. "About six months ago I went to one of the smaller Ryūkyū Islands and stayed at an inn. I was looking down at the people passing under my window one evening when the wife of a U.S. Signal Corpsman stationed there walked by carrying her baby. She stopped to talk with four or five teen-age boys from the neighborhood and let them take turns holding the child. I don't know if this could happen in Okinawa, but it did not seem unusual on that small island. Still, I was very surprised."

His little story seemed rather pointless, but I realized that Ogawa, too, wanted to express his relief.

Mrs. Miller smiled radiantly as she walked toward us, and I noticed that her cheeks were charmingly flushed. It might have been the shock of the child's disappearance, or perhaps her cheeks reddened when she drank. In any case, their color made her seem all the more alluring. I suddenly found myself imagining Mrs. Miller taking a moment while she taught English conversation to ask some of her adult students about their children. And I began to wonder if some of the men in her class felt guilty, excited by her voluptuous figure.

AFTERMATH

It happened on that same hot and humid night. Unable to locate Mr. Morgan's boy, you and Mr. Sun had stopped at the metal fence surrounding the family brigade. About the time you were listening to his recollections, your daughter was being attacked at Cape M. She had already gone to bed when you arrived home, mildly intoxicated, from the party. Your wife greeted you, her face tightly drawn, and showed you the school uniform your daughter had worn that day. From the many rips and stains it was obvious that something terrible had happened to her, and the sight filled you with horror.

She had been raped by Robert Harris, the American soldier who rented your rear apartment. Three hours before her ordeal you had sauntered through the security gate into the family brigade feeling smug because you could walk around inside without the slightest worry. While you were looking for Mr. Miller's house, your daughter had been on her way home from visiting a friend. She had just reached the edge of town when Robert Harris called to her from his car. The two of them, the tenant and his landlord's daughter, rode along casually, stopping for dinner in town, then drove out to enjoy the cool of the evening at Cape M. The cape is an ideal place to escape the heat at night, but it is twenty-five miles from town, and even the nearest village is two miles away. They had seen no one else around that night, and it was there that he suddenly turned brutal.

You were grateful not to have heard the details directly from your daughter, but for the rest of the night you almost couldn't believe it really happened. First of all, Robert Harris already had a girlfriend. In fact, it was because of her that he had rented the apartment where they could stay together two or three days a week. As a tenant he'd always been friendly with your family. Recalling pleasant chats you'd had, you couldn't imagine his attacking anyone. Of course, you were aware that such incidents occurred in these postwar times, but it was difficult to connect the vaguely sinister image of alien soldiers with the foreigners you knew personally as friends.

His girlfriend returned to the apartment the following day after having spent about ten days with her family on another island. You told her what happened, though neither you nor your wife had considered what to do about it. Accusing Robert Harris, pressing charges, seeking compensation—such things had not yet come to mind. You told her simply and directly, without raising your voice or showing emotion. At first, only her eyes revealed the shock. After you finished, she sat silently for a moment, then cried out all at once in a voice filled with anguish.

"He's made both of us his victims!"

She immediately began to pack her belongings, and by the next day she had moved out. You assumed she would seek refuge with some of her friends, but if she intended to break up with Robert Harris, she left no message to give him when he returned. You felt then how remote this girl's world was from your own. Yet at the same time you were struck with an acute realization of the suffering Robert had caused, and rage welled up inside you. By the third night after the incident, you were determined to press charges.

Your daughter, however, strongly opposed prosecution. She wouldn't say why, though at first you assumed it was because she felt ashamed. You sympathized with her, but the crime and Robert's situation with his girlfriend remained unresolved. You could no longer bear the feeling that you were always surrounded by a world beyond your reach, so you tried to persuade her to change her mind. She insisted that she was not objecting out of shame; and when you pressed her, several times she seemed on the verge of revealing why, but in the end she refused to tell. Then, on the following day, you learned the reason.

The house was visited by a foreigner, accompanied by a Japanese-American interpreter. They had come to take your daughter into custody. Apparently, following the rape, she had pushed Robert over an embankment, and he'd been seriously hurt. The issue now did not seem to be Robert's attack on your daughter. According to these men, who said that they had been sent from the military's Criminal Investigation Division, she was to be arrested "on suspicion in connection with an injury to U.S. forces personnel." Robert Harris, "the injured party," was now in a military hospital. You hurriedly explained that she had acted in legitimate self-defense, but to no avail. They only suggested filing a separate complaint. When you asked if this should be done at the C.I.D., they said to go to the Okinawan police station. Then they took your daughter into custody.

Once you and your wife were left alone, a dark and oppressive atmosphere seemed to infiltrate the house. Neither of you ate that day, and she cried bitterly as she recalled what had happened or stared fixedly into space with horror in her eyes. You tried hard to imagine where your daughter might have been taken. You knew that in Okinawa the American C.I.D. and the Okinawan police comprised a two-track system of criminal investigation and that the C.I.D. handled matters relating to the military, but you had not the slightest idea of how its investigation would proceed. Of course, you had never witnessed an Okinawan criminal investigation, either, and could only assume it was something like what happened in mainland Japanese detective stories and films. Still, at least you knew what an Okinawan police officer looked like and could feel some familiarity with the local police station and police headquarters. In contrast, everything about the C.I.D. and the C.I.C. was an enigma. Once you and a friend had speculated casually about where their headquarters might be, but even this remained a mystery. Now you wondered if they also had jails somewhere.

You tried to picture what was happening to your daughter in custody, but some impenetrable barrier seemed to block the flow of your imagination. She had been taken into a world no one could speak freely about, so you could not envision it. Recalling the men who led her away, you thought it strange that they had looked so ordinary, and you realized with wrenching sorrow that you had no idea how they might interrogate her. How much easier it would have been if parents' attendance were required, but obviously it was not. Then, if only they would let her claim legitimate self-defense or, at the very least, would make allowances for her psychological state at the time.

You went to the city police station to begin the procedures for filing charges.

"I'm sorry to hear that," said the middle-aged police officer. He seemed genuinely concerned. "Where is your daughter now?"

As you explained rapidly how she had been taken into custody by the C.I.D., you felt a driving urge to act, to do anything, even if it were only spewing forth a long stream of words.

"...so surely her state of mind after such a vicious assault must be considered."

"Well, there will be an opportunity to investigate all the circumstances. Frankly, I don't like having to tell you this now, but you must try to understand."

Despite his ominous introduction, the officer's explanation did not sound unreasonable at first. You could see why your daughter's rape and Robert Harris's injury would be treated as separate incidents. His trial would be held by the army and her case would come before the Government of the Ryukyu Islands district court. It also seemed logical that she had been detained by the C.I.D. to expedite investigation after Robert filed a complaint with the military. In any case, the officer said her custody would probably be transferred to his office. You understood this, too, recalling that the bureau you worked for, though called "governmental," actually fell under the jurisdiction of a higher government. What he said next, however, completely took your breath away.

The court-martial would be held in English. And since rape is the most difficult crime to prove, there was absolutely no chance of winning the case. It was standard procedure to advise against pressing charges. The vast majority of complaints filed in the past had been dismissed. Furthermore, it would also be impossible to prove the defendant's claim of self-defense because the Okinawan judiciary had no authority to summon U.S. military personnel— such as Robert Harris—as witnesses.

His words swam inside your head, and your voice broke as you tried to speak. "You mean...we're just supposed to bear this in silence?"

"Well, we don't like to put it that way."

At this point the officer switched to a familiar bureaucratic tactic. Instead of answering your questions directly, he simply began to repeat the same explanation. You quickly interrupted him.

"So our courts have no subpoena power. But suppose the witness agrees voluntarily to testify?"

Now the officer looked surprised.

"Well, if it's voluntary..." He seemed to want to add that this was inconceivable.

"Then I'll get him to testify."

"You will?"

"That's right. I'll arrange it. Then if we prove legitimate self-defense at the trial, can't we expect a conviction from the court-martial?"

"No. The court-martial is still a separate matter." There seemed to be a trace of sympathy in the officer's eyes. "It's not really legitimate self-defense though, is it. You've already said that his injury occurred afterward. To plead mitigating circumstances is different from claiming legitimate self-defense. That's what I tried to tell you before."

Now thoroughly confused, you could barely follow what the officer was saying. A void of darkness seemed to hover before his eyes. Your memory flashed back ten years to that afternoon you had gotten lost trying to find the east end of the family brigade. As you walked in frustration along winding streets that seemed to lead nowhere, Okinawan maids and gardeners, your fellow countrymen, had cast furtive looks at you. What sentiments had been radiated in those glances—suspicion, scorn, resentment, compassion, or disguised indifference? Surely the feelings of the officer who sat before you now were different from any of these, but he shared one thing with the others. They all seemed to cry out in silent despair "there's no way we can help you."

Then all at once you recalled the happiness you'd felt just a few days before, hurrying to the cocktail party after the guard had waved you through the security gate. And now the family brigade's neatly paved streets, almost deserted on that hot and humid evening, seemed to offer you a way out of that despair. The memory of walking to the party revived you.

"I'll arrange it," you said again. "The witness will appear in court without fail."

"I see," said the officer without changing his sympathetic expression. "Then we'll file the complaint as soon as you succeed in bringing in the witness."

* * *

You telephoned Mr. Miller and asked urgently to see him. He agreed at once and invited you to his house that evening after work. You reminded him to inform the guard of your visit and felt a sense of relief when his animated "of course" came over the phone. His voice still retained the mood of the party, and it seemed only natural that you should meet at his home.

When you arrived, Mrs. Miller was at the door with her husband. You thanked them for the party and they replied that it had been most enjoyable for them, too. After these initial pleasantries, you felt entirely at ease talking with them.

"I was wondering," said Mrs. Miller, "why your daughter has missed English class the last couple of times."

Her question presented a perfect opening and you immediately began to explain what had happened. You were hardly surprised to see them frowning uncomfortably, and simply continued your account. Presently Mrs. Miller got out of her chair and slipped quietly from the room. When she had gone, you told Mr. Miller the name of Robert Harris's military unit, as you had remembered it, but added that he was probably still in the hospital. Then you asked if Mr. Miller would accompany you there for a meeting with him.

"He must be persuaded to testify in court."

"This is a rather sudden request," said Mr. Miller. "In all my experience, this is the toughest thing to deal with."

"I'm sorry. I realize this will seem to pit you against another American, but I had to ask someone. I don't even know if they'd let me into that hospital alone."

"They would if you went through the proper procedures."

"Even so, do you think I could succeed in convincing him by myself?"

"That depends entirely on him. So why should it make any difference if you go alone or with someone else?"

"It's not that I'd be going with just anyone. But with you, an American."

"This is most unfortunate. The incident could easily lead to a serious confrontation between Americans and Okinawans."

"It already has."

"No, I don't think so." Mr. Miller eyed you sharply. You tensed. "Basically, it's something that happened between two young people. Of course, you are also involved as the girl's father. But, after all, this sort of thing can occur anywhere in the world. Thinking of it as an injury to Okinawans only complicates the problem."

"What do you mean?" The back of your neck was beginning to feel warm.

"That's what I wanted to ask you. Why do you single me out to help you condemn the act of one young American just because I also happen to be an American? That doesn't make sense to me."

"Is going to the hospital too much trouble for you?"

"Perhaps not. I wonder, though, if it wouldn't be better to talk to him yourself. If this Robert Harris were someone I knew, I could see some point in going. But he's a complete stranger. I hate to mention this now, but we've worked hard to build friendships here that transcend race and nationality. And I believe that together we've established equality in our relationships. I wouldn't want something like this to destroy the balance we've worked so hard to achieve."

"I don't understand. If something has been damaged, we can fix it later. But right now I need your help. I only thought having you along as an intermediary would be better than a one-on-one confrontation."

"Well, then, how about Mr. Sun? A lawyer ought to make a good mediator. And since he's neither American nor Okinawan, his position is ideal."

"Would it be so unpleasant for you to face the shame of another American?" You stood up as you spoke.

"This may sound rude." Mr. Miller also rose out of his chair. Then he continued, choosing his words carefully. "But I have no evidence that Robert Harris did anything shameful, and I'm in no position to judge him. Maybe you can prove otherwise. With Mr. Sun."

"I see. I'm sorry to have bothered you." You turned to leave.

"Wait. Don't get the wrong idea. Let me repeat that I've worked hard to build good will here. I don't like to seem uncooperative, but we must avoid conflict among Americans if we are to preserve our friendship with Okinawans. I want you to understand that."

"I'll try, if I can."

What kind of understanding was he talking about? Would Mr. Sun know? Or Mr. Ogawa? Maybe if you had brought one of them along, they could have persuaded Mr. Miller to go to the hospital. You had gotten as far as the door.

"Oh, leaving already? What did you decide?" Mrs. Miller called after you. "I do hope the shock hasn't been too much for your daughter." The soft skin above her neck caught your eye, and all at once you remembered a certain ordinance from American occupation law in Okinawa:

> Any person who rapes, or assaults with intent to rape, any female United States Forces personnel may be punished by death or such other punishment as the U.S. Civil Administration court may order.

You thought of a hypothetical case to which the ordinance might apply, with Mrs. Miller as the victim and you as her assailant. How would Mr. Miller feel then, you wondered, and how would Mr. Sun and Mr. Ogawa react? You tried to imagine what sort of upheavals the case would provoke in Okinawan-American relations as you walked slowly along the neatly paved streets inside the family brigade. Recognizing a clump of bushes from the night of the search for Mr. Morgan's boy, you pictured this as the scene of the crime, but your imagination would take you no further. In the distance the security guard could be seen performing his monotonous duties. You knew now that you would have to ask Mr. Sun for help.

* * *

"Do you think I was betrayed?" you asked Mr. Ogawa at his apartment, having decided to go there first for a talk with him.

"It's probably better to see this as your first test in a long ordeal," Mr. Ogawa replied quietly. "There's a perfectly logical reason for Mr. Miller's behavior, though it must have seemed incredible to you."

"I feel more mystified than angry. At first he acted just like he had at the party. Then, when I asked him for help, he suddenly turned cold and businesslike. Since I started meeting Americans, I thought I'd gotten pretty good at talking with them using their kind of logic."

"Yes, but haven't you noticed that, for them, the logic of friendship is something rather abstract? I even felt it at the party the other night. Although we'd all been invited as equals, there was still a considerable gap between them and us. Of course, the two groups mixed later, but this was because of something unusual, the disappearance of Mr. Morgan's son."

"Yes, I'm well aware that there is often a kind of boundary line at such parties."

"It's probably the result of self-consciousness on both sides." Ogawa stood up and walked across the room. When he returned he handed you a small memorandum book. "This is the list of members of the American-Okinawan Friendship Council. I never bothered to look at it until just a few days ago, during the hundred and tenth anniversary celebration of Commodore Perry's landing in Okinawa."

You quickly spotted a line and gasped in surprise. "Here's Mr. Miller's name. Occupation: Army Counter-Intelligence Corps!"

"That's right. So this is the first you've heard of it."

"You mean we've been seeing him all this time and didn't know what his job was?"

"Only because he never told us. How did you first happen to meet him?"

"He came to my office, saying he'd heard from someone that I could speak Chinese. And he asked if we could meet regularly and talk."

"That's exactly what happened to me. Isn't their intelligence network remarkable! I wonder what other secrets they know about me!"

Ogawa chuckled, but for you this was no laughing matter.

"So he works for the C.I.C."

"I asked him what his job was at least twice," said Ogawa.

"So did I."

"Come to think of it, he dodged the question both times, and I carelessly let the matter drop. He did say that he'd learned Chinese in the army, though."

"That's what he told me."

"You learned it at the academy in Shanghai. I was born in Peking and studied later at the Tokyo University of Foreign Languages. But why would they teach someone Chinese in the American army? Maybe for postwar pacification or intelligence? Still, that wouldn't explain why he doesn't like to tell people what he does."

"Many of the guests we met at the party told us their jobs as soon as they introduced themselves. Mr. Morgan started an argument with you, but he seems now like the more honest of the two. It's ironic, isn't it?"

"He seemed calm, compared to Mr. Miller, even when his boy got lost, though I wonder now how real Mr. Miller's concern was. There's something wily about him that I never noticed before. And I call myself a reporter."

Ogawa paused briefly before continuing.

"During the Allied occupation of Japan, I heard about a minor American official who learned Chinese because he was keeping a teenage mistress in Hong Kong. I let this memory prejudice me and assumed Mr. Miller had also learned it this way. It never occurred to me that he might have studied Chinese for intelligence work."

"Yet you did bring up Kuo Mo-jo's novel at the party. And you told Mr. Miller that he should respect a great writer even if he is a Chinese Communist."

"I remember mentioning Kuo, though I don't recall going so far as telling Mr. Miller to respect him."

"Did you learn about his job after the party?"

"No, before. That was our first meeting after I discovered it. I wanted very much to confront him with the information as soon as I arrived, but I felt as though it were caught somewhere in the back of my throat. Even after several drinks I could barely manage a few cynical remarks."

There was now a slight commotion on the stairway outside Ogawa's room. You recalled that the first floor of his apartment house was a cafeteria where the tenants, mostly single men, ate their meals.

"Won't you have some supper with me?" he asked.

"No, there's something else..."

"Of course. Let's telephone Mr. Sun later and perhaps we can visit him tomorrow."

"I wonder if he'll help me."

"Are you afraid he'll take the same attitude as Mr. Miller?"

"No, but I'm thinking he may be my last hope."

"Then how shall we approach him? As a lawyer whose cooperation we need?"

"Asking will be awkward, but I think it would be better if he agreed to help as a friend."

"All right."

"Quite honestly, between the two of them, I turned more naturally to Mr. Miller because he is an American and I feel he knows me better. I can still remember walking through the family brigade without the slightest apprehension because I thought I could rely on him." You continued to chatter away foolishly, though Ogawa could not possibly understand how you had felt. "I assumed he would be the more sympathetic to my situation, but after what happened today, I can see that Mr. Sun is actually much closer to me. Perhaps I'm being selfish."

"No, not at all. Let's try telephoning him later. But how about some dinner now?"

"No thanks. Really. At this point I don't want to make my wife eat alone."

* * *

The next day you visited Mr. Sun's home for the first time. Having made an appointment by telephone, you arrived with Mr. Ogawa a little past nine in the morning and found Mr. Sun outside in his garden. He was already back from playing golf and had just finished breakfast, he explained as he pruned his hibiscus. The bright clusters of red petals looked moist and fresh.

"They're really beautiful," you exclaimed, momentarily forgetting why you had come.

"In Okinawa they call this 'the flower of the next world,'" said Mr. Sun. "In Hawaii the hibiscus has a romantic image. Perhaps the notion of life after death it symbolizes here is also romantic."

Mr. Sun lived alone and employed a middle-aged widow as a maid during the day. His home was not part of the government-built base housing but in one of the projects with rental units for foreign tenants that competing Okinawan construction firms had begun hastily erecting some three years before. The approximately five hundred houses, which seemed to creep up the hillside in long rows, were coated in an array of colors according to each builder's tastes. Yet no matter how they were painted, their grainy concrete sidings always seemed to show through. The project looked dreary from a distance, but driving up the hill that morning, you noticed that it was not surrounded by a fence and seemed open to anyone, unlike base housing. Mr. Sun's home was at the very top of the hill. After getting out of the car, you turned to gaze back down at an expanse of pure blue sea far below and the highway that stretched in a white band along the shore. The scene was dazzling to the eye, like an oil painting.

Now, as you watched the crimson blossoms tumble from Mr. Sun's pruning shears, which made a short scraping sound as he cut, you suspected all at once that he had lied when he said his wife and child were still alive on the Chinese mainland. It seemed far more likely that he had left for Okinawa only after he knew they were dead. And, for some strange reason, it became easier to broach the matter on which you had come.

According to prearranged plan, Ogawa had agreed to open the discussion, but this was no longer necessary. As you began to explain, you felt that Mr. Sun was someone you could talk to about anything. Ogawa stood by silently, gazing at the wall where a Chinese landscape painting hung. You know very little about art, but this soot-stained picture, its sweeping strokes of India ink marred here and there with rips and smudges, looked quite old, and stood out conspicuously in Mr. Sun's neat, bright, Western-style living room. Mr. Sun listened quietly, but his eyes seemed especially alert, looking directly into yours without blinking. You were exerting every effort to avoid any possible confusion in the thread of your story.

"So I gather that what you want me to do...," Mr. Sun interrupted himself to drain the last bit of cold coffee from his cup, "is to persuade this injured party to appear voluntarily as a witness at your daughter's trial."

"*We* are the injured party," you said, almost shouting.

"All right, then let's call him Mr. Harris. But you're not asking me to be your daughter's lawyer, are you?"

"I haven't decided about that yet."

"The language in an Okinawan courtroom is Japanese, so I'm afraid I'm not qualified. And I hope you won't misunderstand me, but do you think I'd have any chance of persuading him to testify if I weren't acting as a lawyer?"

"If you're suggesting I hire an Okinawan lawyer, no American would listen to me."

The figure of Robert Harris lying in bed at the military hospital flashed into your mind. If he was able to file a complaint, he must certainly be conscious. You wondered where he'd been hurt when he fell. Could it have been his head? his leg? Even this remained a mystery. Perhaps his injury had been fabricated. Or a slight scratch might have been exaggerated. If so, then you were being deceived brazenly and contemptuously.

"I'm not an American either," continued Mr. Sun. "How much difference do you think there is between a Chinese and an Okinawan in the eyes of an American?"

You could not tell whether he was trying to be ironic or appealing to some notion of camaraderie. You replied while still in doubt.

"Americans clearly think of themselves as our rulers. They see you Chinese as neutral third parties."

"Yes, I suppose that's true to a certain extent. Well, I'll try to persuade Mr. Harris. But what will you do if we can't get him to agree?"

It was a question you could not answer.

"If he consents to appear as a witness now, it would mean he'd be willing to reveal exactly what he did to your daughter. I'm afraid he isn't likely to risk that."

"Are you telling me to give up before we start?"

"I hate to say that. Still, I think it would be better not to press charges."

"But Mr. Sun, this was rape! My daughter and I aren't afraid of a judgment when it comes to his injury. The point is that such an attack as he made on her should never be condoned."

"I understand how you feel. And that's why you must think very carefully. When the police said your claim would be difficult to prove, they only meant that your daughter would certainly be deeply scarred psychologically by repeated trials."

"So you're also telling me there's no precedent for winning."

"Perhaps some cases are won. But for you it is not a question of winning or losing. Surely the welfare of your daughter is more important. In using his injury to accuse her and conceal his own crime, your adversary has already proven his ruthlessness. So, faced with your accusation, he would say anything to deny the charges. Do you think your daughter could endure rigorous cross-examination before a court composed entirely of American judges, lawyers, and prosecutors?"

Now you remembered that she might be undergoing interrogation by the C.I.D. or the police at this very moment.

"How many days does a trial take?"

"A fair trial requires time. Of course, the old Japanese army and the Chinese Communists always found it easy to pass judgment right away when the case involved Chinese people."

The words "old Japanese army" stunned you momentarily, but you managed to regain your composure.

"It's not the trial itself, but the fairness of the whole judicial system here that I question. They want to hold a court-martial apart from an Okinawan government hearing in which the judge has no power to summon the prime witness because he is a soldier. Can you call that justice?"

"Listen, if we start talking about the military bases here, you and I are bound to get into an argument."

"Why should we? I'm not a Communist. I understand why the present international situation requires American bases in Okinawa. But don't you think this is a separate issue?"

"A little while ago you pointed out that I was just a neutral third party here. This means, unfortunately, that I have no voice in local politics. You probably think my life is secure because I have a law practice and residence status. But these privileges are extremely fragile. Compared with you two, I have to be much more careful of what I say."

When he had finished speaking, Mr. Sun turned to look at the landscape painting that hung on his wall. Now you finally realized what he was trying to say. He wanted you to know that he had consented to help persuade Robert Harris only with great reluctance. Still, you could not understand why he needed to be so wary. Wasn't prevailing on Harris a perfectly legal undertaking? And, besides, wasn't this really a matter of conscience quite unrelated to politics? Then again, was he afraid that involvement in the case might make him party to a breach of military secrecy because of Harris's army job, something you and your daughter knew nothing about?

As Mr. Sun continued to gaze at the landscape painting, you reflected on the difficulty of his position. Separated from the nation of his birth, he was forced to rely on his skills as a lawyer to make a living on Okinawa's military bases. This alone would be enough to make him uneasy. Furthermore, he lived in an area of more than five hundred houses with people from various countries; but most of the residents were Americans, and he probably felt like an outsider. Perhaps this was why he spent so much of his time gazing at ancient art objects from his homeland. He loved the hibiscus flowers on this island but kept his distance from the people here.

You recalled the day you were first introduced by Mr. Miller and the many times you had met Mr. Sun since then and talked about your experiences as a student in China. You'd known him for three years, but was it really just an accident that today was your first visit to his home? Maybe you didn't qualify for admission into Mr. Sun's solitary, private world. And perhaps, even after three years, your relationship wasn't strong enough for him to help you in such a personal way. To you, it seemed now as though Mr. Sun were receding into the mists surrounding a distant mountain in that landscape painting. Feeling nearly total despair, you turned to Mr. Ogawa.

"Under the circumstances," Ogawa began without looking back at you, "we came to ask for your help as a friend."

"In that case..." Mr. Sun switched his gaze from Ogawa to you. "I'll go to the hospital and do whatever I can there."

He almost seemed to be speaking these last words to himself, as if to bolster his resolve for the task ahead.

* * *

The receptionist said Robert Harris did not want to see you.

"This is extremely urgent," Mr. Ogawa insisted. "If his condition permits it, we must have a word with him."

After a time, the doctor in charge, a mild-mannered older man, came out to the waiting room. "It's only a fracture of the right leg, so his life is hardly in danger. But there hasn't been time for recovery since his operation. It would be unwise to excite him. If you'll promise me ... "

"We'll do our best not to excite him," said Mr. Sun.

You were shown to a ward brightly lit in white where about ten Caucasian patients lay in their hospital beds. Seeing Robert Harris in the far corner, you felt strangely relieved.

"I can guess why you're here," he said as soon as he saw you, then turned to Mr. Sun. "Are you the Japanese lawyer?"

"Chinese," answered Mr. Sun.

"Chinese? Oh, that's right." He looked back at you. "I heard you could speak Chinese." It seemed incredible now that Robert Harris should know anything about your personal life. "You mean a Chinese is going to defend her?"

"I'm not defending anyone."

"Then why do you want to talk to me? Can't you see the people in this room are patients? You have no right to upset them."

"Of course not. Nor do we have any right to put you under legal duress. That's not why we're here." Mr. Sun's tone was composed and deliberate. "We ask only that you join us for a calm and reasonable discussion."

"We'd both agreed to it. Then afterwards she turned on me."

"Would you testify to that in court?"

"What?"

"Look, we're not accusing you of anything. But this man's daughter is under indictment awaiting trial. Won't you testify at her trial?"

"Testify to what?"

"You just said that, after acting with her consent, you were betrayed. But she claims she never agreed and that you have committed a crime. Although you are under no indictment, this is a serious accusation. Unless you testify, people in Okinawa will think that you ... "

"That's a lousy trick and it doesn't fool me one bit. The fact is your daughter broke my leg, and I don't have to appear as a witness in any Okinawan court."

You tried repeatedly to put in a word only to be restrained by Ogawa tugging at your sleeve. Anger and despair rioted inside you. It was hard to believe that this patient before you was the same Robert Harris who had rented your rear apartment for his girlfriend and stayed there with her a few days every week, the same boy who often met and spoke with your family in his halting

Japanese. Occasionally he'd talked about his own family and their farm in California. You'd even had the illusion of knowing them. It seemed unlikely that even an actor could change his personality constantly to fit whatever role he was playing at the moment. You remembered reading an essay on drama claiming that a person's unpainted face isn't necessarily his real face; you had assumed that, if this were true, it pertained only to the world of the theater. If it also applied to everyday life, which was Robert Harris's real face? And what was his true relationship to your family? You never asked whether he and his girlfriend were legally married, but they certainly seemed devoted to one another and made a handsome couple besides. You had once imagined them riding together in a yacht that glided majestically over the waves. And now . . . to your own daughter . . . this hideous, shameful act.

"Have you seen your girlfriend?" you asked.

"That's none of your business."

From his curt reply it was impossible to tell whether he was angry after breaking off with her or simply trying to brush aside any further questions.

"You have the right . . . ," began Mr. Sun, but you interrupted.

"This is no longer a question of rights and obligations. Let's go." Then, as Mr. Sun and Mr. Ogawa turned toward the door, you faced Robert.

"You said you acted with her consent. Well, I didn't believe it for a minute. Now you've confirmed my suspicions."

* * *

At Mr. Sun's suggestion you walked together along a roundabout route through a nearby golf course instead of heading straight back to town. No one wanted to play golf, but to sit and talk for a while on the soft grass. In the midafternoon heat only a few people were out with their clubs. It was nearly summer, and watching their flowery "aloha" shirts flutter in the breeze made you conscious of how much they seemed to be enjoying their lives that day.

"I did the best I could." Mr. Sun seemed again to be speaking half to himself, but now there was a defensive note in his voice.

"Thanks for making the effort," you answered. "I probably should have pressed on with it, but I just couldn't bear any more talk about legal rights and obligations."

"I understand how you feel. Still, you must remember that these two words have acquired a kind of mystical power during the troubled course of human history. Unfortunately, nowadays they are often a lawyer's only means for resolving disputes."

"Not in this case. The rights and obligations that should apply don't exist in Okinawa."

"I don't like saying that even bad laws are laws, but for us lawyers they're all we have to work with."

"Why not tell us what you think of American occupation law," broke in Mr. Ogawa. "Not in a courtroom, but here."

"Because, as I have already told you, I am only a third-country national."

"Then how about speaking as a Chinese instead of a third-country national?"

"What do you mean?"

"Your country was ravaged by Japanese soldiers who occupied Chinese territory. Doesn't this help you appreciate what people in Okinawa are going through now?"

Mr. Sun stared intently at Ogawa, and you were startled to see his face darken with a shadow of anger that quickly faded to a look of deep sadness. At this point you wanted very much to change the subject, but it was too late; Mr. Sun had already begun speaking.

"I was afraid one of you would ask me that question. It occurred to me when I first heard about your daughter this morning. I tried to put it out of my mind, but now..." Mr. Sun looked first at you, then at Ogawa. "I'd like both of you to tell me where you were and what you were doing on March twentieth, nineteen forty-five."

You and Ogawa looked at each other. He answered first.

"I was still going to middle school in Peking. On March twentieth I believe I was traveling on our school excursion in Mongolia."

"The year before," you continued, "after graduating from the academy, I'd gone into the army and become an officer. On that day I was probably drilling soldiers on the outskirts of Nanking." As you spoke, it felt almost as if you had come under Mr. Sun's cross-examination and were revealing something suspicious about yourself.

"I was living in W., near Chungking," Mr. Sun began without responding to what either you or Ogawa had said. "I'd planned to move on to Chungking, but we were delayed because my wife got sick. It happened there on March twentieth. That day my eldest son, who was then four, got lost. He'd been playing in the neighborhood with some other children; that evening he didn't come home."

Listening to Mr. Sun, you recalled standing beside him at the fence surrounding base housing. That night under a star-filled sky he had shared a painful memory with you. Gazing then at the neatly paved roadway inside the American family brigade, you had tried to picture Mr. Sun walking along dark streets at night in search of his child. He'd told you his story only two or three days before, but now it seemed like a long time since you'd heard it.

"I must have walked around for about three hours," he continued. "I can't tell you how relieved I was when I finally found him in protective custody at the Japanese military police headquarters. Even if this 'protective custody' were actually kidnaping, there was no room inside me then for anything except gratitude. I walked straight home with my son through the darkened streets. But by the time I got to my house, my wife had been raped by a Japanese soldier."

"What?!" you called out in surprise. "You didn't mention that before."

"There was no need to. Or, rather, I'd hoped to avoid mentioning it, if at all possible."

"But you really wanted to tell us, didn't you?"

"So many things nowadays are best left unsaid, no matter how much we may want to blurt them out."

"Are you saying we shouldn't press charges now because your own wife was raped by a Japanese soldier?" asked Ogawa.

"No, I'm well aware that two wrongs don't make a right." Mr. Sun looked at Ogawa with a certain gentleness in his eyes. Ogawa ignored it.

"Then you're a coward. Especially after what happened in China."

"I suppose that's one way to look at it," Mr. Sun replied. "As long as you're talking in the abstract, it's easy for you to compare America's occupation of Okinawa with Japan's occupations in China and to condemn what the Japanese did there. But if you really hope to understand these things, you need to recall more precisely what contacts were like between Chinese and Japanese from the time you lived in China yourself. On March twentieth you were traveling in Mongolia. Try to remember how the Mongolian people acted toward you. What sort of relations did they have with the occupying Japanese soldiers?"

"I was barely in my teens, but I'd say the Mongolian people were very kind—at least to us."

"Do you think their kindness was sincere?"

"I wouldn't know."

His last question brought to mind an experience from the time you were still in training. It had been eight months before March twentieth. The midsummer heat on the Chinese mainland was fierce, and, walking on maneuvers, some of the troops liked to drag their boots through the water in rice fields beside the road. On the march that day you and a buddy had straggled behind, just as glad you couldn't seem to catch up with the rest of the company no matter how hard you tried. In this rear area far from the battlefront, no one felt any sense of urgency.

You came upon a single farmhouse along the road. Your throats were dry and both your canteens were empty, so, without even thinking, the two of you walked in and demanded water. A middle-aged couple were alone in the house. They hurried into the kitchen at once, brought out two large bowls of chilled rice pudding, and presented them to you with deep bows as if they were making some sacred offering, though you must have looked to them like a sorry pair of Japanese troopers. Knowing that all their bows and friendly smiles were put on made you feel acutely inferior. You both gulped down your fill of the delicious pudding, finishing the two bowls, and after muttering a single word of thanks in Chinese, trudged off again. As you headed up the road, you wondered if the old couple were whispering about you.

"But I . . . ," began Ogawa, before Mr. Sun cut him off.

"You probably want to say you didn't do anything wrong yourself. You criticize the way the Japanese treated people in China. Yet when this was happening right before your eyes, you pretended it didn't concern you."

"Maybe so, but the attitude you're taking here today amounts to the same thing," Ogawa replied.

"I admit that. Still, I must point out how each of us is guilty of this shameful hypocrisy." Mr. Sun turned to you. "You were an officer. Did you keep close enough watch on the behavior of your trainees toward Chinese civilians?"

"That's a coward's ploy!" shouted Ogawa. "What happened then doesn't excuse your lack of courage now."

"Of course not." Mr. Sun was on the verge of tears as he spoke. "But did it take courage to ignore what was happening all around you in China?"

You sat in silence, feeling quite incapable of arguing with Mr. Sun. You remembered one of your troops who had stolen something from a Chinese peddler. Filled with indignation, you had strongly reprimanded him, but later the company commander bawled you out for overreacting to the incident. And, though confident of having done the right thing, you said nothing. Perhaps this had occurred on March twentieth. Still, you were sure that this past negligence didn't mean you had lost the right now to accuse the perpetrator of this vicious crime against your daughter. Yet you remained silent.

"Did you keep close enough watch on your trainees?" Mr. Sun's question echoed in your ears together with an ominous pronouncement. "Even if you prosecute Harris, it's hopeless." At this point, a terrible loneliness seemed to shut you off from the others. Somewhere inside you another voice protested that the two incidents were unrelated, but you could only shake your head.

"Look over there." Mr. Sun pointed at two people walking some distance away. "Can you see that American and Okinawan? They seem to be together, but we can't hear what they're saying, so they look somehow alienated from one another. Just like us."

The three of you stood up.

Later, walking along, Ogawa whispered to you. "Don't give yourself a guilt complex. This has nothing to do with us during the war."

But as he spoke, you recalled the party and his mention of Kuo Mo-jo's novel *Waves.* He had referred to a scene in which a Chinese mother chokes her screaming child to death when she hears the roar of Japanese warplanes overhead. You had added that such things happened during the Battle of Okinawa, but couldn't bring yourself to elaborate. Now you remembered wanting to say that there were instances of Japanese soldiers bayoneting Okinawan infants inside caves where their families had taken shelter.

Again you were unable to speak the words in front of Ogawa, whose relatives quite possibly had fought as Japanese soldiers in Okinawa.

* * *

After everyone went his separate way, you headed straight home. A short time later, just as your wife started making dinner, your daughter showed up. She walked through the front door and barely glanced at the two of you with a faint, cold smile. She had never greeted you like this before, and it was a shock. From her manner you sensed that what she had been through would change your lives irrevocably. Yet you thought it very strange that, for someone who had just undergone two full days of interrogation, her face had lost none of its color and her dress looked as clean and pressed as it had the morning she left home. During her absence you had been unable to sleep, trying to imagine what sort of questioning she was being subjected to, and you had also discovered a wall around Mr. Miller and Mr. Sun that you never thought existed. Now, the anxious desire to know what your daughter had been through quickly overwhelmed your relief at seeing her again.

Her story astonished you and your wife. She had apparently been questioned until late in the evening, but was released without having to spend the night. She was told that her custody was being transferred to the local police station, but instead of returning home she went to stay at a friend's house. Her friend, she explained nonchalantly, was a former classmate who had moved to Koza City several months before and transferred to another school. Anyway, she hadn't really wanted to come back. She had never before stayed out overnight or wanted to be away from home, but she said she had dreaded the thought of being in the house where her parents would gaze at her sadly from morning 'til night.

You tried hard to gauge her feelings as she continued. It occurred to you that Koza was a town full of bars and cabarets, and you wondered what kind of friends she had made there. For a moment you suspected she was not telling the real reason she decided to stay out overnight. But you soon realized that, if she wanted to make up a story, she would hardly have said she dreaded the pitying looks of her parents and spent the night in Koza. And now it annoyed you to have harbored the same twinge of mistrust toward your daughter that you had felt toward Mr. Miller and Mr. Sun. When she finished, you told her how, during these past two days, you'd gone to Mr. Miller and Mr. Sun for help in persuading Robert Harris to testify, and planned to accuse him while he was on the witness stand.

"No! You mustn't!" she cried out in alarm.

The next day you took her to the city police station. The middle-aged policeman you'd spoken with before questioned her for almost two hours while you waited in the next room. When he finished, he said she was no longer under any restrictions. Then he explained that the case would be sent to the prosecutor and wanted to know if you had hired a lawyer. Finally, he asked if you still intended to file charges against Robert Harris. You looked at your daughter, who was staring down at the floor, then turned back to the policeman and hung your head low. You would not press charges at this point, you told him.

* * *

It was with a crushing sense of futility that you later telephoned Mr. Sun and Mr. Ogawa. Mr. Sun said you had made the right decision and promised to advise you fully during your daughter's trial. Ogawa claimed he was not surprised you had changed your mind and asked if it wasn't really better that way. He obviously wanted to chime in once he assumed the matter had been settled. You told no one else of your visit to the police station.

Your daughter started going to school again. Fortunately, news of the crime didn't leak out while you waited for the district attorney's investigation and the trial. People were sure to hear about it eventually, but you and your daughter summoned your courage, confident that her actions that night had been above reproach. Even the anger and disappointment you felt toward Mr. Miller were beginning to fade. Then, a few days later, Ogawa telephoned with a message from Mr. Miller inviting you, Ogawa, and Mr. Sun for lunch the following Saturday at the club on the base. You were reluctant to accept at first, but Ogawa assured you that Mr. Miller probably wanted to apologize, and in the end you decided to go.

You were still wary about starting a conversation with Mr. Miller, but everything went smoothly at first. He had brought Mrs. Miller, who turned to you as soon as you arrived. "I was so relieved to see your daughter back in class and looking well," she said. When you responded only with a half-hearted smile, Mr. Miller turned quickly to Mr. Sun and Mr. Ogawa and began thanking them for coming to his party. You were still thinking about how long ago the party seemed, though it had been held only a few days earlier, when before you realized it the others had launched into a discussion of Okinawan culture.

"My wife told me," Mr. Miller turned deliberately in your direction as he spoke, "that Okinawan culture was the most interesting thing we talked about the other night. I went right back to the museum to learn more about it."

Unsure how to interpret his obvious effort to act as if he had forgotten your last meeting, you decided to give a perfunctory reply.

"Even we Okinawans disagree about the connections among Okinawan, Chinese, and Japanese culture."

You began to wonder how many centuries this debate would continue unresolved, and you remembered what Mr. Sun had said about the two men—one Okinawan and the other American—you had seen walking together on the golf course. Then all at once someone called out from close by.

"Well, here you are. All together!"

You turned and saw Lincoln, the bright-looking young man you'd met at the party, hurrying toward your table. He pointed at each of you, one after another, and exclaimed, "Now this is a perfect example of international friendship!" Hardly pausing for breath, he continued. "Hey, remember how worried everyone was about Mr. Morgan's boy the other night? Well, Mr. Morgan's brought charges against his maid."

"What? Really?" You banged your fork noisily against the side of your plate.

"That's right. I heard about it from a friend who works at the C.I.D. They're investigating and she's been called in for questioning. It would be a shame to charge her if she's innocent, but suppose she really had intended to kidnap him? They couldn't just let her off."

You looked first at Mr. Miller, then at Mr. Ogawa and Mr. Sun. All three of them had fallen silent and were wearing grim faces. Only Lincoln retained the jovial atmosphere of the party, but what he had just said obviously reminded everyone of your daughter. Now you were certain that Ogawa had guessed correctly why today's meeting was so hastily arranged. Mr. Miller had invited everyone here on short notice after your visit to his home in an attempt to mollify you.

"It sure was a strange night. But kind of interesting. That's life, I guess. Well, I mustn't keep my friends waiting. By the way, today's special on the menu is duck casserole. It's my favorite." Lincoln turned and walked around to the other side of the bandstand.

A white man passed in front of you straightening his tie. A foreign couple on the other side of the bandstand were smiling and exchanging greetings with an Okinawan couple who had apparently just arrived. You heard a child's voice behind you and turned to see a family of foreigners at a nearby table. The waitress was trying to serve the children ice cream, but one of them complained that it wasn't what he ordered. The family maid was talking to the waitress in Japanese while the cranky child kept poking the maid in her arm with his finger.

Customers gradually filled all the tables. You thought of Mr. Morgan's maid eating supper at her home with his son the night of the cocktail party. Then you pictured your daughter sharing a table with Robert Harris that same night in town.

"What century did contacts begin between Okinawa and China?" Mr. Miller questioned you abruptly.

"Are you really interested?" You had stopped trying to be polite.

"What?" Mildly flustered, Mr. Miller continued uncertainly. "Well, I only thought we might use this meeting to discuss the history of cultural exchange."

_____: I think we ought to drop it.

Miller: Oh, really? Why?

_____: Because I still can't forget our last meeting.

Miller: But you...

_____: Mr. Sun went with me to the hospital after you refused.

Miller: He did?

_____: You said Mr. Sun was the ideal person to ask, but even he couldn't help me directly with the case.

Miller: I suspected that. It's unfortunate for you, but he's probably better off not getting involved.

_____: What do you think, then, about how Robert Harris treated us—how we were insulted by this American?

Miller: That would depend on what he did, and the circumstances. (Mr. Miller had now regained his composure.)

_____: It reminded me of something that happened in September of nineteen forty-five, just after the war. I had been discharged from the army in August and was living in Shanghai. One day I was walking down a nearly deserted street when a young white boy coming the other way suddenly turned and punched me as hard as he could in the stomach. I was wearing an armband marked 'Japanese resident,' and as I doubled over in pain, I knew for the first time what it meant to lose a war."

Sun: The Chinese were more understanding toward the Japanese after the surrender.

_____: Yes. I was surprised that Chinese troops from the countryside were especially kind. Thanks to them, we felt much less stigmatized as the people of a defeated nation. It made that punch seem all the more outrageous to me.

Miller: Was he an American?

_____: I'm not sure. People from various countries lived in Shanghai in those days, so perhaps he wasn't. But at the time I was certain he was American.

Miller: I don't mean to sound unsympathetic, but couldn't your emotional state after Japan's losing the war to America have caused you to believe that? This emotionalism would also explain why you appear to be taking your resentment of another American out on me now. It seems so unlike you.

_____: Maybe I am being emotional. But Robert Harris was far too objective when he told me he had no obligation to testify at my daughter's trial because the law in Okinawa doesn't require it.

Miller: Sometimes objectivity entails sacrifice.

_____: Mr. Sun told me the same thing, but I wonder if either of you can claim to live according to such rigorous standards.

Ogawa: (in Japanese) You'd better not go on with this.

_____: *(in Japanese)* Thanks, but we still haven't gotten to the main issue. *(in Chinese)* Did everyone understand what Mr. Ogawa just said? He's worried that I'll upset the balance among us. But he knows very well that our whole relationship is based on false pretenses. Mr. Miller, you said you were surprised that I should make you a target because of the way another American treated me. But am I really any closer to you than to other Americans? If so, then why did you deliberately mislead me when I asked about your job?

Miller: I was forced to because of the nature of my work. I had no ulterior motives.

_____: But now that I know what you do here, how can you expect me to believe that? You've put a barrier between us.

Sun: You're going to destroy everything I've tried to accomplish.

_____: Your efforts are commendable, Mr. Sun. The problem is that, for too long, you avoided what had to be dealt with.

Miller: What were you trying to accomplish, Mr. Sun?

Sun: Just before the war ended, President Chiang Kai-shek addressed the army and the Chinese public. He said we would soon win the war, but urged us to make friends with the Japanese once the fighting was over. He reminded us that our enemy was Japan's military regime, not her people.

_____: I also heard that speech. It explains the way the Chinese treated us after the war, though we sometimes took their kindness for granted.

Ogawa: But the Chinese never really forgave the Japanese, did they.

Miller: Of course not. It's impossible, no matter how laudable Chiang's exhortations.

Sun: But we've done our best these past twenty years to overcome our resentment and work for a reconciliation of wartime enemies. And now you've destroyed it.

_____: No, Mr. Sun. Robert Harris destroyed it, along with Mr. Miller and Mr. Morgan.

Miller: That's ridiculous. You don't understand the logic of international friendship. Friendly relations between nations start with friendships between individuals. This is also true of animosities. Inevitably, they arise, but we should always try to maximize friendships. It's the same between people. There might be resentment now, but we can always hope for friendly ties in the future.

_____: It's only a disguise. This great friendship you talk about is nothing but a mask you've all put on.

Miller: It's not a mask. Friendship is something we can always believe in.

_____: That sounds nice in theory. You'd have to get hurt once like I did to see how it only conceals the truth. But now I'm going to end this masquerade.

Miller: What will you do?

_____: Press charges against Robert Harris.

Ogawa: But you'd decided not to.

_____: Only because I was fooled by this logic of masks. I could kick myself for refusing to see how I was insulted and betrayed. But it's not too late. And now I'm going to fight this case through to the end.

Sun: It will only cause suffering for your daughter.

_____: We'll be ready for whatever happens.

Sun: Sometimes people need to wear disguises. You weren't hurt nearly as badly as I was. I put on a mask to ease the pain. If I hadn't, I couldn't have gone on living.

_____: But you finally had to take if off! What you told us the other day sounded like something you'd been waiting twenty years to say. You tore off your mask and confronted us with the crime of that Japanese soldier. I'm only asking for the same chance now.

Sun: It's a chance you're better off not taking.

_____: You were the one who opened my eyes, Mr. Sun. The justice I seek for my daughter is the same you would want for the victims of Japanese occupation in China. I'm sorry I couldn't see that before coming here today, but now we must stop deceiving ourselves. It isn't just the crime of one American that I want to indict, but all the pretense of the cocktail party.

Miller: You're going to make a lot of people unhappy.

_____: Mr. Miller, are you familiar with articles two and three in the criminal code under section two of ordinance one forty-four?

Miller: Articles two and three?

_____: Please read them later. They are the procedures to be followed in cases of rape against U.S. forces personnel. All your fine hopes come to nothing so long as such law exists.

You left the club. Outside, a huge banner was stretched across the street in front.

> PROSPERITY TO RYUKYUANS
> AND MAY RYUKYUANS AND AMERICANS
> ALWAYS BE FRIENDS.

This was the toast Commodore Perry delivered in 1853 at an official reception for him in Okinawa. The banner had been hung about a week before the cocktail party as part of the 110th anniversary celebration of Perry's landing. You took a long look at those words, then turned and walked toward the police station.

* * *

A month later an investigation was under way at Cape M. Your daughter had been named defendant in the case of Robert Harris's injury, and you were given permission to accompany her to an on-site inspection. Cape M. was entirely too peaceful. The four or five tourists who usually came with their fishing rods were nowhere in sight that day. The area was deserted except for a single bonito fishing boat that drifted far out on the open sea. The melancholy splashing of waves against the coral reef below the cliff was the only sound. To reconstruct in this landscape an event so peculiarly human seemed ludicrous. You were seized momentarily with a crushing despair that made you want to lie down and beat the ground with your fists, but somehow you weathered it.

The judge had instructed your daughter to identify the scene of the crime. You had not been permitted to attend the prosecuting attorney's earlier inspection, and you worried now because she was being questioned again. Perhaps some discrepancy had arisen between the two investigations. Robert Harris had refused to appear in court, and there were no witnesses to corroborate her story, so she would have to testify alone throughout the trial. She wore a one-piece dress, and her hair fluttered in the breeze as she responded to an interrogation that spared none of the details of the incident. She traced an imaginary Robert Harris with her hands in the air and moved from the ground where they had rested to the site of the crime and then to the place where they had struggled. You watched while she tried her best to answer questions that seemed unduly probing and repetitive. At least one more on-site inspection would be necessary to prepare her case. For the trial she needed irrefutable testimony that would overwhelm Robert Harris's accusation.

She had said nothing when you told her you had filed charges. Her silence affected you strangely. You explained at length why it was necessary to prosecute, describing what had happened in China twenty years before, wondering if she could possibly understand. Your wife, who sat anxiously beside you, asked why you needed to bring up something that had occurred so long ago. As your daughter continued her silence, a note of apology crept into your voice. You imagined the anguish this decision would cause her and began to feel pangs of regret. You were determined not to let your emotions betray you. Still, you wondered why she should have to suffer in the name of justice for a crime that had been committed in China before she was born. The question had probably not occurred to her; she seemed concerned only about how long her ordeal would last. And, even when it was over, you knew she might lose both trials.

You tried hard to imagine what she was going through now. What were they trying to prove, you wondered, by making her reenact the whole episode over and over again? As you scrutinized her movements, you attempted in vain to connect her ordeal with your past negligence and your present outrage. You still found it incredible, not only that this peaceful landscape had been the scene of a crime, but that this person called Robert Harris could actually exist, even as you watched your daughter trace his figure in the air. Perhaps the landscape itself was an illusion. It was just as Mr. Sun had said about the scenery in certain areas of his homeland. We become oblivious to the natural environment when our lives are filled with crisis.

Yet at that moment the scenery on Cape M. seemed strangely vivid. Your daughter stretched one of her light-brown arms out over the cliff and held the other above her head. In the background was a sea so blue it seemed to soak into the pupils of your eyes. She might have been reenacting the moment of desperation when she pushed her tormenter over the cliff. In the ocean a white bank of wave crests glided toward a distant reef. You stared at your daughter and held your breath, praying that she would be able to fight her case openly and vigorously at a trial attended by Mr. Miller and Mr. Sun. In that courtroom there would be no illusions.

.

Child of Okinawa

Higashi Mineo

Child of Okinawa

Higashi Mineo

1.

I was asleep when Mom started shaking me. "Tsune. Tsuneyoshi, wake up!"

"Huh?"

Rubbing my eyes, I poked my head out from under the covers and looked up at her. She brought her smiling face down close and spoke coaxingly.

"Michikō and Yōko picked up a couple of soldiers, but there aren't enough beds. Won't you let them use yours, Tsuneyoshi? It will only take about fifteen minutes."

I was startled at first, then revulsion welled up inside me.

"Not *that* again!"

When Dad opened a bar for American soldiers at our place, I never thought I'd have to lend them my bed. Michikō and Yōko had made the alcove next to the bar into a bedroom. It was nearly filled with a double bed where they took turns sleeping with their customers. But if they both had customers at the same time, Mom would come into my room. This didn't happen very often, but when she woke me I was supposed to cooperate.

"Let them all use one bed together," I said, sitting up.

"Don't be silly! Now hurry or we'll lose this chance to make some money." Mom unfolded a starched sheet as she rushed me out of bed.

"This sure is a lousy business you're in."

"There's no use complaining. It's how we eat, you know."

"It's still lousy."

It made me want to cry, thinking people would probably do anything to eat. I took my school cap and satchel off my desk and pushed them under my bed out of sight.

"Excuse us," said Michikō. She came into my room leading a soldier by the hand. As she put her arm around his waist, she glanced at me with a faint smile.

2.

And now they were in my bed, doing it like a couple of dogs. If I stayed in the house, I would still hear the moans and squeaking bedsprings, so I dashed outside. Then I took off down the hill toward Koza Primary School.

"Tsuneyoshi! Where are you going at this hour?"

In my rush to get away, I had run right into Chiiko, my forehead smacking into her breasts, just as she came out of the Yamazatos' doorway.

"I'm out for some jogging."

"Your hair is an awful mess. Better get it cut tomorrow." She scolded me like a big sister as she fixed her skirt. I didn't think my hair was any of her business, and ran off without answering. But I stopped after a few steps and turned back to look at her walking along the road up the hill. In a way I was glad she had spoken kindly to me.

Above the hill I could see the whole sky, lit up by the pale glow of neon. Chiiko's skirt spread like a parachute, and her slender legs poking out under it reminded me of a hopping sparrow. Suddenly, to my surprise, a soldier standing on one side of the street stepped toward her. She grabbed his arm, and, walking together, they turned a corner out of sight.

3.

Koza Primary School is a little building crammed into a narrow valley. Beside it is a playground so small it looks more like someone's backyard. The surrounding hills are thickly overgrown with *susuki* grass, but jutting from their peaks are naked limestone rocks that seemed to pierce the night sky. Poisonous *habu* snakes thrive in those hills. The valley was so dark I could hardly make out the white lines on the hundred-meter track trampled over daily by the children. Panting and weary, I stretched out to catch my breath on the square wooden platform where the teachers led morning assembly. I seemed to be looking up at the sky from the bottom of a well. Out here, only the stars lighted the sky overhead, and the breeze felt good as it dried my sweat.

4.

When I got back to my room, it was filled with a strong, woman's odor that made my nose feel stuffed up.

"Mom, my watch is gone!" The watch, with Popeye's picture on its face, was a present from Chiiko.

"Did you take it somewhere?"

"No. I hung it over this nail, right here on the wall."

"Well, then, it must have fallen off."

Mom came in wiping her hands on her apron. A few grains of rice tumbled from her apron. All I could see on the floor was a trickle of douche water.

"No, damn it. It didn't just fall off. I *told* you this was a lousy business."

There were white droplets at the corners of Mom's mouth, so I knew she had been chewing uncooked rice again. She told us not to eat it because we might get worms, but she munched on it herself now and then.

"What kind of a son are you—always complaining. Don't you know what Dad and I go through for you kids?"

She was always talking about how parents toil and suffer for their children. Hearing this over and over again made me want to leave home and stop being a burden to them once and for all.

"All right, then. I'll quit school and go to work."

"Sure, you just try finding a job with no education. You'll end up in the fields carrying a manure bucket."

5.

Later that night I dreamed about a typhoon. I was peeking out the front door and could see the raging wind tear the thatched roof off our goat shed. Inside, the goats bleated as the rain beat down on them. They reared against the door and yanked at the ropes that bound them by the neck, almost choking themselves.

"Tsune, shut the door right now before that wind blows in here!" Mom ordered, but I couldn't take my eyes off those goats being pelted by the rain. Their bleating sounded to me like desperate cries for "f-e-e-d, f-e-e-d." Afraid they would starve unless I ran out to cut grass for them right away, I was in agony, like when I had to go to the bathroom real bad. And it got worse and worse until I began groaning in my sleep. At last, just when I could stand it no longer, I woke up. I was relieved to find myself lying in bed, but felt strange to discover tears around my eyes.

6.

What made me have such a dream, I wondered. More than a year had passed since we raised goats at Misato village in the nearby countryside. Besides, we would never have gone out to cut grass for them during a storm. We always prepared ahead for typhoons by cutting big piles of grass and tossing the goats an extra supply. When the winds came, they would crouch down for cover, quietly chewing their cud. Remembering them now, my relief turned to loneliness.

Two of our goats had been shipped from abroad as something called "commodities aid." One of them was a chestnut-colored female with big brown eyes. When she stood up, I could see her drooping udder that was large enough for one of the white goats born here in the islands to hide behind. Her horns grew out in coils until the tips grazed the skin behind her ears. One day Dad shortened her horns with a hacksaw, but he tried to cut one horn too low, and sliced into her flesh. I felt sorry for her as she winced in pain with the blood trickling down. Hugging her neck to keep her under control, I shut my eyes tightly as Dad began sawing on the other horn.

Soon after that, the prettiest little chestnut kid was born, though I guess all animals are cute when they're small. Then one day I went out to cut the goats some grass and found him lying dead where he had fallen into a manure pit next to a neighbor's field. For a while his mother dripped milk wherever she went. She never bore another kid.

After grandfather's death, we sold our house and moved to town. We also sold our goats to someone in the village, and since the female couldn't bear kids anymore, she was probably soon killed and eaten. But whatever became of her had nothing to do with me now that we lived in town. So why was I worried about her? Anyway, I knew I should go back to sleep because I had to get up at five in the morning for my newspaper route. I'd started working part-time to bring in some extra money for us. Maybe the strain of my new job had caused me to have that dream.

7.

I can still remember the day we moved to town. We piled our bureau and fly curtains, blackened by kitchen smoke, onto a truck with our grimy mattresses and mosquito netting. I couldn't help feeling embarrassed as we rode along the military highway in the bright afternoon sunlight. It seemed funny, but sad too, and I'd wanted to laugh and cry at the same time.

On the military highway—so wide that everyone joked it was also built for airplanes to take off and land—passed cars driven by American women and buses packed with local people. Signs in English lined both sides of the road: SOUVENIRS, RESTAURANT, TAILOR SHOP, HOTEL; and passing soldiers danced to music drifting from bars and cabarets.

This was the city where we would make our new home. From my window I could see a loudspeaker mounted on the roof of a movie theater. American popular songs echoed all through the town, and even in the daytime women carrying their washbasins walked by on their way to the public bath.

Dad drifted quickly through a series of business ventures.

"Here in town we should be able to make a nice profit," he said. Then, after his noodle shop and grocery store both failed, he decided to go into the bar business. He talked to Mr. Yamanouchi who managed one of the many bars on "Gate Street" which ran from the entrance to a big air force base through the center of town. Dad listened carefully as Mr. Yamanouchi taught him his trade.

"You have to choose girls with queen-bee figures, big tits and slim waists. Get three or four of them and you're in business. If you can find one like our Suzy with white skin and a nice round ass, you'll really rake it in."

People said Mr. Yamanouchi had made so much money he used a bureau for a cash box. Dad followed him everywhere. They went to hire a carpenter, to look for girls, and to get a commercial license at the town office.

Then one afternoon when I came home from school, the girls had arrived. From the sound of their laughter, I could tell they were already busy in the bar. Dad was talking to Mom with his mouth full of food.

"See, you make loans to the girls who bring in lots of money. That way they have to keep working for you to pay off their debts. Of course, nobody lends money to the girls who can't sell, so they just drift around from bar to bar."

He talked so matter-of-factly about women who are lured into debt and then held like slaves. How could he sit there and gossip about their misery while chewing his food with such pleasure? I stared at his Adam's apple bobbing up and down.

8.

"Tsune. Tsuneyoshi, get up." Mom shook me awake. That was how every day started for me.

"What, five o'clock already? Ugh, that smell again. It always stinks like perfume in here."

"Tsune! Hurry or you'll be late for your paper route."

Morning again. I sprang out of bed, remembering that Dad said I should rise like a Japanese soldier in the true samurai spirit. Dad had gotten up early himself and was reading aloud from yesterday's newspaper, beads of saliva forming at the corners of his mouth. His voice boomed out excitedly, as though he were making a rousing speech. He liked to show off to Mom, who couldn't read. Meanwhile, she hunched sleepily over a pot of miso soup that was steaming on the kitchen stove.

No one would be out this early, so without bothering to wash my face, I quickly slipped on my sandals.

"Shouldn't you take your account book?" Mom asked.

"People complain if I go around collecting bills in the morning."

"But in the evening they'll say it's a bad omen for their bars. Better take it now."

I still had unpaid bills left over from last month, and they were all from places where it was very hard to collect money. A friend had given me his paper route because I promised to take over these accounts.

9.

I felt the damp morning mist and the chill of the wind as I ran out on the street. Up ahead lay what seemed to be a brightly colored handkerchief. I didn't plan to take it, but when I stopped to lift it with my foot for a closer look, I was startled to see it was a woman's panties. Under them, a little dry spot stood out starkly on the wet pavement.

The bookshop where I picked up my newspapers was run by a man from Hateruma, one of the smaller Ryūkyū islands. He was outside sweeping the front sidewalk, and today, as always, he had a toothbrush in his mouth.

"Good morning," I said.

"Morning."

Inside, the store was crammed with books, magazines, stationery, and notepaper. I hurried across the narrow dirt floor to the back door, where my share of newspapers had been stacked, and stuffed them under my arm.

"Has Keizō left already?"

"Yeah, he's gone. Oh, Tsuneyoshi, the Yoshidas' boy picked up their paper on his way to work and left money for the bill."

"Thanks."

10.

"Hello, I'm collecting for the newspaper."

"What newspaper? I've never seen it."

"I leave it inside your front door every day."

"Oh, we don't use that door. There's a bureau behind it."

The man facing me looked like a bartender. He went back into a room reeking with perfume and came out grasping a handful of yellowed newspapers.

"See, all you did was stuff them behind the bureau."

"I'm sorry. I didn't know it was there."

"From now on put them in through the kitchen door."

"All right, but..."

"But what?"

"Your bill..."

"I'll pay it next month."

I looked back at his house as I was leaving and stuck out my tongue. On my way to the next place I had to cross a stone bridge over a stream that had become as filthy as a sewage ditch. Broken glass was scattered all over the bridge's narrow pavement, leaving almost no place to walk. It looked as though someone had smashed a whiskey bottle in a drunken rage. If the glass hadn't sparkled in the morning sunlight, I would have stepped on it.

11.

Later, on my way to school, I saw two classmates walking just ahead of me.

"Keizō!" I was so glad to see him that I ran up to them like an eager puppy. But Keizō barely glanced at me and kept talking to Seiichi, our class monitor. It made me feel bad.

"You were late for your paper route this morning, weren't you." he said finally.

"Yeah, I overslept." I played up to him, scratching my head sheepishly as if to apologize for being late.

"Hey, there's that smell again."

"What smell?" I asked.

"Don't you recognize it? That's the smell of sperm." Seiichi laughed.

Little piles of crushed petals lay on the street. Looking up, I saw that they had fallen from white flowers growing on the branches of a tree overhead. Keizō jumped up to tear off a leaf and began chewing it, wrinkling up his nose. I jumped up too, plucked off another leaf and tried chewing it. It tasted bitter and had the smell of unripened buds.

"Smells like sperm, doesn't it," said Keizō.

"Sperm?"

"You mean you don't know about that yet? You're 'way behind. Tell you what. When you go to Hateruma's bookshop today, look up the word 'sex' in the dictionary. I bet you'll find it interesting. That's 's-e-x,' see?" Keizō traced the word in the palm of his hand.

"You're horny," I said.

"Yeah? Well, don't tell me you're not. Look!" he shouted angrily. "When you point a finger at me, your other three fingers are pointing straight back at you. That means you must be *three* times as horny!"

I'd never meant to say anything to make Keizō turn on me like that. Now I felt like crying. We both liked art and had become good friends, but these days he was always talking to Seiichi about math. That bores me, so as soon as I got to school, I went into the bathroom. I was still in there when the first bell rang for Monday morning assembly; soon I could hear the students breathing hard as they ran out to the schoolyard.

12.

Later, at the end of home-room hour, our teacher, Miss Asato, walked over to our desks on the boys' side of the class.

"Takeshi, I want you to come to the faculty room at recess. There's something I'd like to ask you. And Tsuneyoshi, you come with him."

I didn't know why she wanted to see us, but it was the first time I'd been invited to the faculty room at middle school, and I felt honored.

When we got there, Miss Asato came right over and motioned for us to follow her outside. She led us to a spot behind the school building, next to a banyan tree. Then she put her hand on my shoulder, pulling me away from Takeshi, and peered down at me earnestly.

"This morning someone stole all the class membership dues from Natsuko's school satchel. Do you know anything about this, Tsuneyoshi? You didn't come to morning assembly, did you? Were you late?"

"No, I came to school with Keizō and Seiichi. I was in the rest-room when morning assembly started. I stayed there the whole time."

"I see."

Some schoolgirls from the classroom next to ours came running toward the banyan tree. They jumped up to grab one of its branches that hung down like an elephant's trunk, worn smooth by the many young hands that had grasped it.

"Look, a gorilla!" shouted one of the girls as she pointed toward a wire fence surrounding a nearby field. Inside was an American military radio tower. The MP on guard, a black soldier, was standing with both hands clutching the wire fence. He looked at the girls and sneered.

"Tsuneyoshi," said Miss Asato. "Someone saw a boy with long hair sitting in Natsuko's seat during morning assembly. He was resting with his head down on her desk to hide his face."

"Well, if you think that was me, you're wrong."

How could she suspect me of stealing money just because I had long hair? I stamped angrily on a small shrub that grew up from the rocky soil, then smeared the ground with its green pulp.

"Natsuko's still crying about it. She's assistant class treasurer, and everyone's membership dues come to a lot of money."
"Who told you he saw me? I'd like to have a talk with him."
Miss Asato looked at me silently for a moment.
"Never mind, Tsuneyoshi. I'm sorry. You can go now."
When I got back to the classroom, Masao, the class treasurer, was reading a comic book in the seat behind me while another student peered over his shoulder. I wanted to read it too, so I tapped Masao on the arm and saw him reach up to cover his shirt pocket with his hand. There was money inside! He must have known why the teacher called me out and now he was trying to hide it. I felt trapped. It was bad enough that Miss Asato suspected me of stealing, but with Keizō being so unfriendly, I had nowhere to turn. School had become unbearable. I jumped up and fled from the room.

13.

I scrambled up a hillside grown thick with *susuki* grass and found the underbrush trampled down into a narrow, tunnel-like trail, perhaps by a stray dog. "Tsuneyoshi, come back to school! Don't play hooky again today."
I was imagining that Miss Asato had come chasing after me.
"No!" I called back, crawling up the hill through that tunnel as if to escape her. I was nearing the top when all at once from deep inside me rose a buoyant feeling so strange and powerful it brought tears to my eyes. My heart pounded as I scurried through the rustling leaves and came out suddenly into a bright clearing. I stopped here, thinking I might have to go to the bathroom, but for some reason the front of me had stiffened and nothing would come out. In the distance I could see Katsuren Peninsula reaching out into the ocean like a huge hand. Tsuken and Kudaka islands seemed to be fleeing from its clutching fingers. Standing on tiptoe, I could make out Misato village, nestled just this side of the farm fields below, and the small fishing hamlets that dotted the seashore beyond. Two of the hamlets were separated by an abandoned runway where American soldiers liked to race their motorcycles up and down.
Standing way up here, I felt as if I were floating in the sky. I reached down and began rubbing myself as children sometimes do, but this time a strange and delightful feeling welled up, like one

I'd had before in a dream. When I looked down, a juice that smelled like unripened buds was falling on the grass.

Now I knew the truth. All you had to do was rub yourself. You didn't really need a girl if you wanted to have this good feeling. And what about the soldiers? Couldn't they have it this way too? I felt as if I had just drunk my fill of water after a long thirst and lay down with a sigh to rest on the grass.

14.

Huge columns of billowing clouds rose over the Pacific horizon that stretched out in a long line dividing the sky from the ocean shimmering in the heat of the sun. Beyond that horizon lay island paradises—the riches of Australia, and Saipan where I was born. No one eats papayas in Saipan. They're for the birds to peck at. People eat bananas fried crisp and sweet. How I wanted to go back there! I shut my eyes tightly trying to bring my dim memories of Saipan into focus.

All day long I had played in the shade of big trees with the native children. We made clay models of war planes and battle-ships, then lined them up in rows under the house to dry. We also swam in the ocean. Mom laughed one day when I told her I had gone swimming holding sand in both hands.

Later, to escape shelling from a real warship, our family fled into the jungle. I carried a pile of blankets on my back and held chickens under both arms. Their heads bobbed worriedly as I ran along, trying to keep up with the others. After the fighting ended and we came out of the jungle, I saw skeletons that were still wear-ing clothes lying all over the place.

But I didn't want to think about the war now. To take my mind off it, I pulled a book of maps out of my school satchel and opened to a page where the Pacific Ocean currents are marked by red arrows. As I traced the path of the stream running up from the equator, an idea occurred to me. The current bounced off the Phil-ippines, veered northward, and ran alongside Okinawa before flowing out to the open sea off Shikoku. Then, from Ogasawara, it plunged back down to the South Sea islands. So why couldn't it carry me there? If a boat can float downstream on a river to the ocean, surely I could sail the Japan Current to the South Sea islands.

A puppy was whining somewhere. At first I had thought the sound was coming from the village below, but now it seemed much closer. I wondered if a den of stray dogs might be nearby. From where I sat, the narrow tunnel through the underbrush continued down the other side of the hill. I began crawling through it and, all at once, came face to face with a dog that looked like a hyena, baring her teeth. Startled, I began to edge backward, but saw that she was also backing away. So I stopped in my tracks and waited until she turned and ran off. In her den close by I found plump, furry puppies lying one on top of another, and smelled a strong odor of fresh milk and afterbirth. I chose the largest of the pups and stuffed him under my shirt.

Later, the puppy and I were fast asleep when I awoke suddenly, remembering my paper route. I scrambled down the hillside and, cutting across a burdock field, noticed many strange-looking white objects stuck between the wide, green leaves. Wondering what they were, I pushed the leaves aside and was shocked at what I saw. The sewage pumped out from town must have overflowed onto the field here, and floating in the slush like huge maggots were countless used condoms swollen with air. I imagined that each one still coiled with lust and felt the front of my pants begin stretching like a tent.

15.

When I got home from playing hooky, Chiiko and Michikō were talking in the next room.

"I took off my slip, but when I turned around to look at him, he was crouched in the corner trembling. So I grabbed his cock and asked, 'WHATSA MATTER?' He said, 'I'M SCARED. MAYBE YOU HAVE V.D.'"

I'd know Chiiko's voice anywhere.

"What's V.D.?" asked Michikō.

"It's venereal disease in English. For a kid he had a lot of nerve accusing me of that. So I told him, 'LOOK, I SHOW YOU,' and opened up my legs real fast right in front of him. Ha, ha, ha!"

How exciting Chiiko's voice sounded to me! Strong and sweet.

"What happened then?"

"He got down on the floor, crawled under my legs like a snake, and ran out. He was probably still in high school. Skinny as a beansprout."

"But most Americans have big bodies, so they reach puberty early, don't they?"

"They sure do. I used to work as a maid for a staff sergeant's family in the Zukeran Housing Area. The Muellers were nice people, but their little boy was an awful nuisance. After he turned twelve, he started opening the door when I was going to the bathroom and came in to peek at me in the shower, pretending he had to wash his hands. It got so bad that one day when his mother was away at a meeting, I grabbed him and taught him the facts of life."

"Weren't his parents mad when they found out?"

"I didn't care. Hell, I learned all about that when I was fourteen. Not from Sergeant Mueller, though. It was the old man at the house where I worked before. I kind of wanted to get back at him so I taught that kid real good." Chiiko paused to greet Mom as she came in.

"Chiiko, I thought you'd gone to the bath."

"Yeah, but I ran into Michikō there. We started talking, and before I knew it, we ended up back here. Mmmmmm, what delicious-looking sweet radishes!"

"Why don't you stay for supper. I'll make pork and radish stew," Mom said. Then she opened the door to my room.

"Tsune! Did you forget your paper route? I just ran into the man from the bookshop. He asked if you were late getting back from school. And what is that I see under your shirt? Oh, no! Not a puppy. I thought I smelled something funny in here. You took it away before it could even open its eyes. Go put it back where you found it!"

"And if I do, what about the newspapers?"

"Hey, that's about enough out of you. What are you doing lying around in here anyway? You've got *work* to do."

I wiped my sticky hands on my pants and went out.

16.

The man from Hateruma licked his finger as he reached for a pile of department store flyers and slid one into each newspaper. He sold magazines and stationery as well as books at his store, but the money he sent to his son, a university student in Tokyo, never seemed to be enough.

"How much is this book?" I called out to him.

"Which one?" He did not bother to look up from the work that earned him some extra money.

"*The Adventures of Robinson Crusoe.*"

"*Robin*—" Just then a loud crash came from outside on the main street. "What was that? I haven't heard any typhoon warnings, but I swear that sounded like a house just collapsed. *Robinson Crusoe?* Is the price marked on the back cover?"

"Two-hundred-twenty yen."

"So divide that by four."

"Fifty-five cents. Uh oh, I'm five cents short."

"Never mind, Tsuneyoshi. You can pay me later."

"Really?"

"Sure. If it's a book you like, go ahead and take it."

Now there was more noise outside, and people went running out to see what had happened.

"Tsuneyoshi, you don't have time to go gawking. Your stack is finished now, so get started. And don't forget to say 'I'm sorry the evening paper is late.'"

As I hurried down the main street clutching the newspapers under my arm, I ducked and dodged through clusters of soldiers smelling of soap who ambled along or lingered on the sidewalk, and felt like a football player charging gamely toward the goal line. In front of one store, waitresses in shiny, starched uniforms and bar girls in dresses reeking of perfume stood pressed together with soldiers in a crowd that had gathered.

"What a goddamn mess!" I could hear someone shouting, close to tears, and decided to take a quick look. A taxi had overturned in front of a telephone pole, and bits of broken glass were scattered like diamonds on the pavement.

"Those bastards have gone too far this time!" The driver pounded his fist on the twisted front of his cab, and the siren of an MP cruiser wailed in the distance as it sped toward the scene.

17.

I came home starved and dead tired from my afternoon delivery and sat down to rest on the windowsill in my room. Under a pale sky at dusk, the town already echoed with the sounds of another night's business. Engines whined as lines of cars climbed the uphill road, and throbbing music called customers into the bars. I picked up my bamboo flute and started to play.

"Boo!"

I hadn't heard Chiiko come in, and she jumped toward the windowsill, startling me.

"Let me try that." She snatched the flute from my fingers and, not caring that the mouthpiece was damp with my saliva, began blowing it. To tell the truth, I played my flute at the window hoping Chiiko would hear me, but I thought she had already gone to the bar where she worked. Now as she sat close to me with her red-painted lips puckered around the mouthpiece, I felt uneasy. Maybe I was in love with Chiiko only in my imagination. When she gave me back the flute, I did not put it to my mouth again.

"Fish for sale." A woman peddler passed on the street below.

Chiiko placed her hands together on the windowsill beside me and nestled her chin down on top of them. She looked all around my room, moving her eyes in big circles. I hoped she had forgotten about the watch she gave me.

"Did you draw that picture over there?"

"Yeah."

"Hmm. Not bad. Why did you make the whole thing red?"

"Because that's the color of sunset."

"Oh, I see. It's the wagon driver on his way home in the evening, isn't it? So the wagon, the driver, the road, and the hills in the background are all red."

Chiiko turned toward me, tilting her face upward, and gazed at my lips. I remembered sheepishly that I had once hoped she would be the one to teach me the facts of life.

"It makes me feel like painting, too. I'm really good, you know."

"Tsune!" I heard Mom calling from the other side of the door. "Go out and help Naoe draw the water. She already left."

Chiiko seemed to remember something, and a look of sadness passed over her face.

"Mother's calling. You better go."

18.

We get our water from a well more than a hundred feet deep. Drawing the well bucket takes strong arms, so that's my job. Then my younger sister Naoe carries the water in shoulder pails to the kitchen where we pour it into a large copper vat. Watching her stagger along under the heavy load, I wondered if the weight might stunt her growth. I felt sorry for her but didn't want to risk stunting my own growth by carrying it, so I gazed down at the bottom of the well and pretended not to notice her.

"Hellooo!" I called down into the darkness. Far below me a circle of water about the size of the moon was shimmering.

Chiiko didn't see me leaning against the wellhead when she came out of the Yamazatos' doorway with a soldier. He was tucking his shirttails inside his pants.

I always had to draw twelve bucketfuls of water because Mom insisted that we fill the copper vat in the kitchen. Otherwise, there wouldn't be enough water to last through the next day. She helped us pour it; that way she could also make sure we finished the job. She never served us supper until the vat was full.

19.

"It's just *awful*," Mom said suddenly at supper that night. "How will Kōkichi ever cover the loss?"

Dad continued eating. He had hunched up one leg so he could lean over and rest his right elbow on his knee as he wielded his chopsticks.

"And the soldiers ran off without even paying the fare. You think they'll ever be caught?"

Dad was too busy scraping up chunks of fried miso to answer.

"What happened to him?" I asked, no longer able to hide my concern. Kōkichi is Dad's second cousin who drives his own taxi for a living.

"Some drunken soldiers were pushing him around while he was driving, and his cab crashed into a telephone pole."

So that taxi overturned on the main street had been Kōkichi's! Why hadn't I recognized it?

"The soldier sitting in front stamped on Kōkichi's foot and the car went out of control."

"On his accelerator foot?"

"Yes. They were yelling, 'Hurry hurry, hubba hubba!'"

"Kōkichi has two arms. Why didn't he push him away?"

"How could he? There were three marines, big as bulls."

Just then Dad's fist lashed out and smacked me in the forehead.

"Can't you sit up straight?" he shouted.

I'd stretched my legs out under the table and was eating comfortably.

"You've got no manners at all!" Furious, I wanted to ask Dad how he could be so picky when he ate resting his elbow on one knee, but he had already corrected his own posture.

20.

"Tsuneyoshi, wake up!"

"Huh?"

"Come on, get up. You have to go out for more water."

"Water? But I already drew it."

"I had to dump that out. Some soldier thought the cooking vat was a toilet."

"You mean he pissed in it?"

"Yeah. He was drunk."

"Aw, Mom, you should have sent him outside. What were you doing anyway?"

"Hey, don't you know how busy I am—buying beer, boiling water, and what not. I was just wiping the floor after he threw up, and he went crawling into the kitchen on his hands and knees, moaning, 'TOILET, MAMA-SAN, TOILET!'"

"Didn't you yell at him to go 'OUTSIDE'?"

"Of course. I even chased after him, but it was too late. He was already standing over the cooking vat in the kitchen."

"Pissing?"

"Yeah. It steamed up and stank like beer. I shouted, 'YOU CRAZY!' and pushed him over; but he wouldn't stop, and it ran all over the kitchen. I had to pour out the vat, so now you'll have to get up and draw more water. I'll wake Naoe, too."

"I'm not going!"

"Look, it's not even eight o'clock yet. You'll still have plenty of time later to read your book."

"Nope. I've already drawn today's load."

"Hey, you know I can't cook tomorrow without water," she warned, but I stayed where I was.

"Well, then, there'll be no breakfast in the morning. Nothing to eat."

I remained silent and in bed.

"Oh, all right. I'll have Dad go to the well. If he needs help, Kōkichi should be coming back from the fields soon."

21.

This long and skinny town was started by people who lost their land to the American bases. They came to cling along the military highway like ants swarming around a worm that had crawled out in the sunlight. I trudged through the streets sobbing until I reached the wide rows of sweet potato fields just beyond the town's outskirts. Out here dust-covered hedges surround the farmhouses with their pigpens hidden back in the fields.

The moonlight was bright enough to see the pebbles on the dirt road that was a shortcut to the sea, so I wasn't afraid. And as I ambled along the dusty path, the midday heat that still hung in the air made the night feel warm. I found myself caught up in the rhythmic sound of pebbles crunching under my feet, and my tears soon dried. But when I came to a place where the road cuts down toward Yasuda village, for some reason I felt a chill. Trees grew densely along the bluffs on both sides here, surrounding me in darkness. All at once I felt the presence of a demon.

"Guardian spirit, drive it away!" I shouted, and took off running through the darkness, my eyes focused straight ahead. Mom had often told me to chant these words if I were ever really scared; otherwise, she said, my soul would rush out of my body, leaving me senseless. I ran downhill into a small valley where Innomiyado, a refugee camp, had been set up years ago, just after the war.

22.

I remembered seeing long rows of tents in that valley. We had just returned from Saipan, and my grandfather came rushing out of his tent to greet us.

"Zenkichi, Matsukō! You made it back!"

"And you pulled through, too!"

"I heard everyone died in the fighting in the South Pacific. But now you're back! Did the whole family survive the war?"

"Yeah, I held out and didn't go into the army, and we all came through it safely."

"I'm so glad to hear it!"

I had watched the three of them hug each other and cry. I was only six at the time, but it all seemed to have happened just moments ago. Seeing adults cry for the first time had brought tears to my eyes, too. It is something I will never forget. But that was years ago. Mom and Dad never cry or show such strong feelings anymore.

23.

Later, people from Isahama came to live in this valley after their land was taken over for a military base. Now rows of rice fields irrigated with rainwater stretch side by side, separated by ridges of stone and concrete. From the yard of a scrubby little farmhouse beyond the fields came the sound of a dog barking loudly. Even at a distance, I could picture the dog, thin and weak with nerves on edge. I tried calling out affectionately; but, unable to soothe him, I soon tired of his barking and ran on through the village. As I came to the edge of the valley, a gust of wind rose up that smelled of the sea. From here I could see the rooftops of Misato village reflecting dimly white in the moonlight. Beyond them a battleship drifted in the ocean, its patrol lights glaring for no reason.

24.

When I reached the shore, I lay down in a small *sabani* fishing boat drawn up on the beach. The wooden planks on the floor of the boat felt nice and warm under my back. From far offshore came the steady sound of the tide, and the moon seemed to get smaller and smaller as it faded into the west. Overhead, a cool breeze was blowing, but the stagnant air inside the boat attracted mosquitoes that came swooping in from the marshland behind the seawall. Their whining beside my ears sounded like frantic cries for "blood, p-l-e-a-s-e. Blood, p-l-e-a-s-e."

I swatted drowsily, trying to drive them away, when all at once I heard voices. Lifting my head cautiously, I looked out. Looming up on the seawall was the shadow of a man carrying an oar. A second shadow followed close behind of another man shouldering a mast wrapped in sailcloth. They were heading my way, and I was afraid of what would happen if they saw me here. Knowing they might easily take me for a child thief, I imagined one of them grabbing me by the scruff of the neck. Had there only been a sail or an oar left in the boat, I could have put out for the open sea. Instead, I decided to pretend I was sleeping. I lay still as a rock in the bottom of the boat, ready to cry out in feigned surprise if one of them grabbed me.

"And Hamauechi Hiroko, too."

"Yeah?"

The fishermen talked as they waded toward the boats through the shallow water.

"She says she's going to Brazil."

"To marry Seikichi?"

"That's right."

Next I heard splashing sounds as the men bailed water out of their boat.

"Well, she's probably better off. At least she didn't end up like her sister, shacked up with some GI"

"Yeah, wearing those tacky dresses."

"And all that make-up."

Just as I started to enjoy my eavesdropping, their voices faded out. I lifted my head again and saw their *sabani* boat, its little sail now swelling in the breeze, glide toward the open sea. The sky over Katsuren Peninsula had turned purple as morning approached. Out in the ocean, the glaring patrol lights of the battleship had been turned off.

25.

When I next opened my eyes, I was startled to find the sun already high in the sky, baking the skin on my neck and arms. I jumped to my feet, wiping sweat from my neck, and felt the sting of mosquito bites.

The tide had receded far offshore, leaving a dry, sandy beach all around me. For one exciting moment I thought I had drifted to the uninhabited island of my dreams; but looking around hurriedly, I was disappointed to recognize the seawall, washed white by salt spray, and the familiar range of green hills stretching beyond it.

Then I noticed that the fruit knife I kept under my belt was gone. I tended to sleep soundly with my mouth wide open, so someone would have had plenty of time to search me for valuables.

The brightness of the white sand was dazzling. Just for today, I told myself, I would try living like Robinson Crusoe. I set out toward the beach, pretending that this was a deserted island, and began to explore my surroundings.

Countless fiddler crabs seemed to chant curses, spewing tiny bubbles from their mouths while they moved their claws up and down as if to beckon the tide. I launched a surprise attack on their compound. Unable to return to their holes, they dashed around wildly. Some became so confused they couldn't move, while others tried to burrow into holes that were too small and floundered at the openings. Catching fiddler crabs is easy. The one I picked up fit neatly into the palm of my hand and stayed there even when I opened my fingers. It had sparkling colors, with a green back and brown feet. One claw was as big as its body, and glowed with changing hues of green and orange down to a bright red tip. The other claw was yellow and drooped limply. I wanted to take this little critter home but knew that, away from a saltwater environment, it would soon die.

Here and there on the beach the tide had collected in ankle-deep puddles where blowfish foraged for food. I chased after them, determined to catch one, not caring about the water splashing all over my pants. With nowhere to escape, they darted about in quick spurts and hid in the water muddied from the sand I'd kicked up. I had to keep a sharp eye on their hiding places or I would lose track of them. Stepping carefully into their puddles, you can trap one of these slimy creatures under your foot and then grab it with your hand. When caught, a blowfish will squeal and puff out its belly, which will swell up even bigger if you try rubbing it flipped upside down. Blowfish are poisonous, so we can't eat them. Set free, they float in the water like balloons, pretending to be dead, but as soon as you start walking away, they belch out their air and dart away. There's never a dull moment on the beach.

If I turned over the stones that dotted the surface of the tide puddles, I could usually find scissor crabs hiding underneath. They are washed up on land with the high tides, but some of them spend too much time foraging for food and get caught on the beach when the water recedes. Their claws and diamond-shaped shells are covered with sharp spines. Scissor crabs can really hurt you because they will lock onto something with all their might, even if their claws are being wrenched off.

The one I went after opened its claws menacingly as soon as I took away the stone that sheltered it. Decoying those claws with one hand, I snatched its shell from behind with the other. By now I was so hungry that I peeled off the shell, washed the white meat in seawater, and ate it on the spot. But killing the crab gave me a creepy feeling.

Later, I walked out into the shallow water beyond the beach where sea urchins live, their spiny shells lodged among the jagged rocks. I had come here once before with Mom to gather some. She had thrown them back to me on the beach. Then I halved the shells, scooped out the meat with a spoon, and stuffed it into jars. It made a thick, delicious sauce for rice. Remembering the fun I'd had that day, I tossed the one sea urchin I'd picked up back into the ocean. A sea gull glided gracefully overhead, and I was startled to see that I had come all the way to the end of the shallows. The tide can rise suddenly out here, and people playing among these rocks have been known to drown in the swirling waters. Mom told me to watch the direction objects floated on the water's surface to see whether the tide was on the rise. If nothing was floating, she said to spit on the water. I was frightened when I saw my spit bobbing toward the shore, a sure sign of rising tide, and got out of there fast.

In all the excitement I had completely forgotten about my paper route, and now I imagined the scolding I'd get from the man at the bookshop. A black sea slug crawled lazily on the sand. I ran over and trampled it, then watched as it vomited a pure white thread.

If he complains, I'll say I'm quitting. That would make it easier to leave home, I told myself. My courage renewed, I scrambled up the seawall. Yes. And then, after collecting my wages, I would buy a knife, lures and hooks for fishing, vitamins, and whatever else I'd need to live on an uninhabited island. I'd also get books about sailing techniques, nutrition, and the other things I'd have to bone up on for the journey.

26.

September 30, 1659. I, poor miserable Robinson Crusoe, being shipwrecked, during a dreadful storm, in the offing, came on shore on this dismal unfortunate island, which I call'd the Island of Despair, all the rest of the ship's company being drown'd, and myself almost dead.

All the rest of that day I spent in afflicting my self at the dismal circumstances I was brought to, viz. I had neither food, house, clothes, weapons, or place to fly to, and in despair of relief, saw nothing but death before me, either that I should be devour'd by wild beasts, murther'd by savages, or starv'd to death for want of food. At the approach of night, I slept in a tree for fear of wild creatures, but slept soundly tho' it rained all night.

"Excuse me, Tsune. Michikō needs your bed again." Mom's voice interrupted my reading.

"Not now. I'm studying." I frowned without lifting my eyes from the page.

> October 1. In the morning I saw to my great surprise the ship had floated with the high tide, and was driven on shore again much nearer the island, which as it was some comfort on one hand, for seeing her sit upright, and not broken to pieces, I hop'd, if the wind abated, I might get on board, and get some food and necessaries out of her for my relief; so on the other hand, it renewe'd my grief at the loss of my comrades, who I imagin'd if we had all staid on board might have sav'd the ship, or at least that they would not have been drown'd as they were; and that had the men been sav'd, we might perhaps have built us a boat out of the ruins of the ship, to have carried us to some other part of the world. I spent a great part of this day in perplexing my self on these things; but at length seeing the ship almost dry, I went upon the sand as near as I could, and then swam on board; this day also it continu'd raining, tho' with no wind at all.

"Aren't things ready in there yet?" Michikō's voice came from the bar.

"Just a second," Mom called back, then burst into my room. "Tsuneyoshi, hurry up. This will only take about fifteen minutes. Come out of there now!"

"No! You ought to quit selling women."

"Oh, sure I'll quit. Then we'd have to go back to living from day to day. Things would be *ten* times as bad as they are now, and there'd be no money for anyone to go to school."

"So I'll quit school. Then I won't need your money."

"Hey, that's big talk. I won't let you forget it."

I stretched out full-length on my bed and clasped my hands behind my head. Gazing up at the ceiling, I let my thoughts drift back into my own private world.

Robinson Crusoe was lucky. He could take whatever he needed from his wrecked ship, but for my voyage I could bring only the barest necessities.

"Never mind. We'll use the sitting room," Michikō called from the bar.

"Fine. Just let me put away the table in there," Mom called back.

"All right, but please hurry."

"It won't take a second."

I wondered what the barest necessities for life would be. First, I'd need lures, hooks, and lines for fishing. I'd have to live on fish for my whole voyage since I wouldn't be able to bring any food with me. I could get protein from fish meat, calcium from the bones, and vitamin A from the innards. Second, I'd need a large cask of water. Still, even that probably wouldn't last long enough. For rain, all people can do is pray to the gods, but I'd read that drinkable water can also be squeezed out of fish meat. Third, I would need vitamins. I'd read that fish doesn't provide vitamins B or C, and in the old days sailors who didn't eat fresh vegetables came down with beri-beri. Some got it so bad they couldn't walk.

Next door in the sitting room the light went out, and I could hear Michikō calling to a soldier.

"HEY. HEY, YOU. COME HERE."

The fourth thing I'd need is a knife. I'd use it for cooking and, of course, for self-defense. Number five is matches. No, flint would be better. Matches are useless if they get wet.

Deep as I was in daydreaming about my voyage, I found myself distracted now by sounds from the room next door. I heard a belt being unbuckled, loud laughter, and then, as the floorboards began to creak, there were moans and heavy breathing. I could hold back no longer.

I finished so quickly there wasn't even time for me to imagine Chiiko. And when it was over, I wiped myself off with a blanket.

"Where's the hot water for a douche?" Michikō called to Mom.

"Oh, I put it next to the family altar." Mom's voice came from the kitchen where she had been hiding. The light in the sitting room went back on again.

Now I remembered what Mom had said before about being short of money, and I began to worry because I had recently loaned her all my pay from the newspaper route. I went out to talk to her.

"Mom, I have to buy a book, so I'll need that money I loaned you."

"What money?" She busily rolled up the mattress in the sitting room and pretended not to know what I was talking about.

"The twelve dollars from my paper route you borrowed the other day."

"Oh, I thought I'd already paid you back."

I wondered how long she intended to play dumb. Spotting a wet blotch on the mattress, she fled to the kitchen for a rag.

"No, not yet. I know you haven't forgotten about it, either." I followed her angrily into the kitchen. "Well, how about it?"

"What book do you want anyway? You already have lots of school books."

"That's my business. You just pay me back."

"Dad says children shouldn't have money because they'll waste it."

"I won't waste it. Now give it to me!"

"All right. I'll pay you later. Just wait."

"No, I want it *now!*" I was so furious tears welled up in my eyes.

"Listen, I don't have it now. I'll pay you later."

"That's a lie! Pay me now. I want it now!" I ran after Mom, kicking her in the legs.

"All right. Here, take it! You're so stubborn sometimes it makes me sick."

Mom reached into her apron pocket, pulled out the money she had just gotten from Michikō, and threw it down in front of me. Snatching those dollar bills off the floor, I tore them in half. Then I ripped them to bits.

Mom let out a shriek as she reached down to gather up the torn pieces scattered on the kitchen floor.

27.

After that night I was busy every day preparing for my voyage. I went to the library at the Ryukyu-American Friendship Center to read up on sailboats. How they could travel against the wind had always been a mystery to me, but now I learned about "tacking" to windward in a zig-zag course. I also studied pottery making in the encyclopedia. I would need a hobby to relieve the monotony of my primitive existence on a small island, so I carefully memorized the whole procedure:

> First, make a mold from moistened clay soil and set it out in the shade to dry for about ten days. When completely dry, bake it in a kiln at 800° or place it in the center of a fire until it turns red. This will produce a piece of unglazed pottery. To make the finish, crush some quartz into fine slivers, mix them with flakes of bone ash, and add water, stirring the mixture to a thick pulp. After applying the finish, bake the piece one more time to a smooth gloss.

I had never studied so hard before.

28.

A few days later I climbed the hill in front of Koza Primary School to find some flint. After passing a small graveyard, I came to the hilltop where a tank that serves as a makeshift waterworks is mounted inside a hollowed-out rock. I had remembered some time ago seeing glasslike stones packed in the crevice, around the base of the tank.

All around me was evidence of Okinawa's birth in a violent earthquake that had pushed the island up through a prehistoric sea. Waves once washed over the rocks jutting out of the hillside, and now long, jagged cracks remained at the ancient water level. I climbed to the top of the highest rock—battered by wind and spray so long ago—and looked far below to where the prehistoric ocean floor had been. Down there was Koza where I lived today.

From here I commanded a view of the whole town, a jumble of houses clinging along that one military highway. Facing the street were large signboards put up to decorate all the storefronts and to hide everything behind them that was now fully revealed before my eyes. Clotheslines, outhouses, chimneys, and water tanks seemed to be strewn haphazardly among rooftops of rusted tin and soot-stained tile. Piles of trash from "Summer Cleaning Week" lay here and there on the street. Looking down, I wanted to jeer at Koza's shameful side. Then, all at once, I thought I heard someone laughing at me. I looked around, but could see only one man lying face down in the little graveyard I'd passed earlier.

Hollows in the rock where I stood were filled with crumbling white seashells, and I wondered if they might have been there since prehistoric times. After stuffing my pockets with the quartz-like stones I had come for, I made my way back down the hill. I passed an American soldier who stood in the little graveyard, watching his Okinawan girl friend as she picked pieces of dead grass from her hair.

29.

"Tsuneyoshi, Dad's looking for the hammer. Have you seen it?"

I had taken the hammer with me to dig out the flint, and now I went to get it from under my bed.

"I thought you had it. Better take it to Dad. Oh, wait. Your eye looks red. Did you get some dirt in it?"

"Yeah. Feels like sand."

"Well, come put your head down here. Now look up at me." As I lay back with my head in Mom's lap, she took one withered breast in her hands and squeezed out two or three drops of white liquid that dripped into my eye.

"Now blink a few times and the dirt will wash right out."

I sat up from Mom's lap where I had noticed a peculiar smell and looked up at the ceiling. When I started blinking, milk trickled down from the corner of my eye like tears.

"Does that feel better?"

"Yeah, it's fine now."

Outside, Dad was cutting boards from a stack of wood. He wanted to build a fence for our dog Pochi who liked to fetch empty cans, old clogs, mosquito netting, and other junk and scatter it under the house.

"I'm ready to close the fence now," he said. "Go call Pochi."

"Pochi! Pochi! Here, Pochi! Come out of there."

Pochi had grown timid after being hit by a car and spent most of his time lying far back under the house. To coax him out, I poured some miso soup flavored with dried sardines over a plate of rice and brought it out to the yard.

"Pochi, here are some nice sardines for you."

When Pochi came out, his shaggy hair was caked with mud and he didn't smell so good. Now Dad was ready to nail the fence shut, but all that junk was still strewn under the house.

"Tsuneyoshi, get the rake and clean out under there."

"But the rake won't reach."

"Then you'll have to crawl underneath."

"Are you kidding? Through that shit hole?"

"Sure. You can clean that out too, while you're at it. Now get under there!"

I glared at Dad and felt anger rising inside me.

"Well, don't just stand there. Get to work!"

I thought about how the dirt under the house would be damp from all the used douche water that dripped through the floor.

"You better do what your father tells you, young man."

Now I was determined not to budge. I stood with my arms locked behind me around a fence post.

"I will not."

"Why you little smart aleck!" Dad leapt to his feet and swung the hammer he was holding right at my head. Shutting my eyes, I saw sparks fly and wondered if I would die instantly, but he checked his swing and the hammer only grazed my hair. This must be what people mean when they say "just by a hair."

"If you don't mind your parents, you'll never listen to anybody."

Dad always used to say he only hit me because he loved me, but now I knew this was a lie. He hit me when he got angry because he hated me.

"All you've done lately is cause trouble."

As I moved away from the fence post, I cried silently. How could he swing a hammer at my head? He might have killed me. I couldn't stand it anymore in this house where people are treated like parasites. I realized now that Dad was just like the soldiers. All he'd wanted was to get into a woman. Then after he climbed on, something extra had come along. Me. To him I was just a nuisance, a piece of baggage.

30.

For my voyage I wanted a gun, to kill sharks that might attack me or anyone who gave me trouble. Thinking I might like to try shooting someone, I started wanting a gun. Once, years ago, I was cutting grass for our goats in a small grove of trees near one end of the abandoned runway outside Misato village. I had come across a wooden box hidden in the weeds among some gravestones and opened it expecting to find canned goods. But inside, wrapped in oiled paper, were ten shiny rifles. I was so scared at the time that I pushed the weeds back over the box and ran away. Now I decided to go back and see if it might still be there.

31.

From a clear midsummer sky, the sun beat down on the runway. The whole strip was deserted; not even a piece of straw could be seen on the wide asphalt band, which shimmered in the heat. Far down at the other end, trees in the small grove also seemed to quiver, as in a mirage.

Nobody was working in the nearby fields, one of which used to belong to my grandfather. I had purposely come here at the hottest hour of the day after all the farmers had left for lunch, knowing they would rest at home until it cooled off. A lone pigeon drifted overhead, peering down at the fields.

As I trudged along squinting, I could feel the heat of the asphalt even through my shoes. Granddad's field had been under this very spot. I could remember, coming back on the boat to Okinawa from Saipan just after the war, how we all looked forward to eating meat and glazed sweet potatoes when we got to Granddad's house. Then we arrived to find him living in a tent and this runway stretching through his field. Granddad told us it was built in just one week for an attack on the Japanese mainland, but Japan surrendered after the atomic bombings and the attack never took place. Later, the Americans discovered that the salt breeze from the ocean nearby rusted their airplanes, so they abandoned the runway without ever using it. After that, weapons and ammunition were collected from around the area, stacked in huge piles on the strip, and covered with tarpaulins.

Granddad had been one of the people hired by the American military to gather up the ammunition; he was paid in canned goods and cigarettes. After his job was eliminated, he tried farming the shrunken plot that was all that remained of his field. He planted sweet potatoes among the stones that poked up through the rocky soil, but nothing would grow except some shriveled bulbs covered with fuzz that looked more like carrots than potatoes. Now the sight of this field, no larger than our tiny school playground, made me want to laugh.

Mom took over working the field after Dad and Granddad got jobs on the base. My job was tending the goats, and I went out to cut grass for them every day after school. Those rifles I had seen hidden among the gravestones that day must have been stolen from the weapons and ammunition piled on the runway. Later, the piles were hauled away and dumped far out in the ocean.

When at last I found my way to the small grove of trees near the cape where the guns had been, I searched all around the gravestones in vain. I should never have expected them to be here after so many years.

Wandering out to a deserted beach, I saw plovers that tottered along chirping as they made brief stops on the sand. I remembered that, just after the war, this whole beach had been the color of rusted metal from a flotilla of landing craft packed together like flies swarming around a corpse. Then, in no time, salvage workers from Japan had cleared them all away.

From here out to the distant horizon, the ocean gleamed and sparkled with all the colors of a prism. At the White Beach Navy Pier, near the mouth of the bay, a giant aircraft carrier drifted like some huge phantom. Inside the bay, a yacht was floating so quietly I couldn't believe anyone was aboard. I sat down on the concrete seawall, feeling the gentle ocean breeze, and wondered vaguely where I should go next. Though I had no other place in mind, I didn't want to go home.

32.

Soon the heat became too much for me and I also found myself wanting to be around people again, so I left the beach and headed inland to a little fishing village. Its eight low-roofed bungalows were surrounded on all sides by clusters of pine, hibiscus, and banana plants. I trudged along the road through wide patches of shade from the trees, where the cool air revived me, and could hear pine needles rustling overhead in the ocean breeze. Thirsty, I made my way from one island of shade to the next in search of water. The sound of someone planing lumber came from a house where *sabani* boats were made. Through an opening in the hedge I could see a little old man standing under a lean-to roof busily scraping his plane. The keel and inside ribbing of a boat were mounted on the rack beside him.

Behind the house was a concrete tank set up to collect rainwater. I walked over, quickly scooped some up, and gulped it down. The water was tepid from sitting in the tank, but it tasted good to me and I drank my fill. Then, wanting to see how boats are made, I went over to the old man's yard.

"What do you want?" He glared at me in surprise. I noticed that his eyes were red and had no eyelashes. He might have picked up one of the eye diseases fishermen get from diving in the ocean.

"Uh...nothing really. I just..."

"Then you've got no business coming in here!" he roared. I slunk away like a dog hit by a stone.

Returning to the beach I saw a *sabani* boat that had just been painted with preservative and was drying upside down on the sand. I wondered if such a boat could carry me across the ocean. I tried nudging it with my foot, but it didn't move. Then I kicked it hard several times, but it still wouldn't budge. For a small boat, it was surprisingly heavy. As I gave it one last angry boot, the smell of preservative stung my nostrils.

Inside the bay a motorboat circled, leaving a trail of white waves. Beyond it the deserted-looking yacht I had seen earlier was drifting in, perhaps returning from the open sea. Now I remembered that just beyond the fishing village was a yacht harbor used by American employees of the military.

33.

From here I could see the pier, bathed in the waning rays of late afternoon sunlight, jutting out into the harbor. Beyond the wharf, two rows of red buoys marked the channel of green sea-water that had been dug through the shallows. Fourteen or fifteen sleek yachts and cabin cruisers, each polished to a sparkling sheen, were lined up like brothers and sisters along both sides of the pier. I sat down among the pine needles scattered on the cool, concrete seawall and gazed with a sigh out at the sailboats.

There was a guard shack at the entrance to the wharf, and I noticed that the Okinawan guard standing inside carried a rifle. Would he merely yell out, I wondered, if I tried to pass without permission? I put such thoughts out of my mind for the time being.

Seaweed and tiny bubbles floated in with the rising tide and swirled under my feet. The water lapped up under the boats, too, rocking them in a soft and gentle rhythm. I watched a group of children carrying fishing poles as they ran out onto the wharf. They were obviously on their way to fish from the edge of the pier and had passed right by the guard shack. I was surprised to see that the boy leading them was Shigeru, whose older sister, Sachiko, had been my classmate all through elementary school. I yelled out to him.

"Shigeru, wait!"

"Tsuneyoshi!"

I glanced over at the guard in his shack who was now reading the newspaper, his rifle propped up in the doorway. Then I ran out to join Shigeru and his friends as they walked along, munching fried sweet potatoes.

"Let me have some of those."

"Sure, but only the little pieces are left."

"That's all right. We can share them."

I was excited to be so close to the sailboats, gleaming in the sunlight as they bobbed up and down. Someday soon, I told myself. Someday soon.

At high tide the water inside the bay was so still it looked like a huge orange mirror under the setting sun. The lapping of the waves and the rustling of the wind had stopped. Everything seemed to be waiting silently as dusk fell. Then the color of the sailboats, the water, and the hills on the peninsula beyond began changing slowly from orange to a deep red that glowed brighter and brighter until they all blazed with the color of fire. Could this be some kind of omen? We glanced fearfully at one another, our faces crimson, and no one turned to look out toward the buoys again. I held my breath and took in the surroundings. It was as though the last day of the world had come, and, looking up at the sky, for some strange reason I felt like crying.

34.

"He did it because he was mad at Chiiko. He had a terrible crush on her, but she wouldn't go out with him."

"Still, who ever thought he'd toss a grenade into her bar. And now, poor Chiiko. She has burns all over her face."

"I feel awful just thinking about it. And the hot wind from that typhoon's got me down, too. Hey, after we do the wash, let's go to a movie. We haven't seen one in ages. No soldiers will be coming out in this weather."

"Are the storm warnings up?"

"Yeah, didn't you hear it on the radio this afternoon?"

Mom and Michikō were talking as they did the laundry. I tried to sneak past them from behind, but Michikō saw me and alerted Mom with her elbow.

"Ah, Tsuneyoshi! Where have you been?"

I walked into the kitchen without answering, took off my sandals, and headed straight for my room, leaving a trail of white footprints on the freshly mopped floor in the hall. Mom followed after me with soap bubbles still dripping from her hands.

"You're supposed to be in school. What are you doing home now? Did you stay over at Keizō's house last night?"

I had slept on the beach again in a *sabani* boat, and twice during the night I had gone down to look around on the yacht wharf. Now I decided to shock Mom by telling her the truth.

"I slept on the beach."

"On the beach? Oh no, Tsune, you've come under the spell!"

I had shocked her all right, and now I could tell she was really worried about me.

"Don't you know ghosts roam the beach? That's how the Odos' kid drowned out there last summer."

According to a local superstition, drowning victims turn into embittered spirits that prowl up and down the beach until they find someone else to lure into the ocean. Otherwise, they can never rest in peace. Ghosts were probably not to blame, I thought, but dead people did wash up on the beach from time to time. And maybe, in a way, I had come under a spell.

"Those horrible night crows I heard last night. They must have been an omen. I ran out and told them to go away and haunt somewhere else, but you just never know. Tsuneyoshi, please! Eat your lunch right away. I put it under the fly net. Then go straight to school. It won't be too late if you hurry."

In Mom's frantic warnings I could feel her love and concern, but I had made up my mind and nothing was going to change it. I had come home only to pick up the equipment I needed for my voyage. Mom looked at me as if she wanted to say something more.

"It's a shame," she muttered to herself, then walked away.

I hurriedly pulled open my desk drawer and took out fish hooks, string, a knife, vitamin pills, and packets of pumpkin and corn seeds. I stuffed them all into my pockets, which were soon bulging; and when I picked up my canteen, I could see it would never fit inside. The canteen was vital, not only to carry water, but because I needed the compass mounted in the cap. To make a place for it, I emptied my school satchel of books and repacked it with the canteen and all the things from my pockets. I also slipped in the booklet of maps from my social studies text that would be my marine chart. Then, from my bureau, I took out the sheets I would use for sailcloth along with blankets and clothes. And from under my bed I brought out a hatchet and an old rope used to draw water from our well. All these things were essential. Next, going into the kitchen to get an empty flour sack, I saw that Mom had set out a plate of stew and rice for me on the table in the sitting room. She was now in the backyard with Michikō hanging the wash.

"Yōko, aren't you going to the bath?" Michikō called.

"Yes, in a minute." Yōko walked through the hall, carrying a mop and pail. Spotting my white footprints, she squatted down to wipe them up. She wore a very short skirt, and her head covered with hair curlers looked like a beehive. She glanced over at me, but I ignored her as I put my school satchel and the flour sack on my desk.

When the girls had left for the bath, I went out into the sitting room and began wolfing down the stew and rice as fast as I could.

"Tsune! You should never eat standing up. It's bad manners. Better start behaving yourself or Dad will smack you again."

Mom was glaring at me from the kitchen. Her face, bathed in sweat, looked gaunt and weary. She carried the rice pot into the sitting room and set it down beside the table.

"Should I warm up the soup?"

"No, it's fine."

"I can see that's not going to be enough for you. Just wait and I'll go buy some eggs to fry."

Mom picked up her shopping basket and hurried out. As I watched her leave, I choked back a sob. I had firmly resolved to end my dependence on Dad, but at that moment I couldn't even swallow my food. Now, at this crucial time, I felt myself wavering. I stood up and walked back to my room where I took a long look at my school satchel and the flour sack lying on my desk.

"No!" I whispered. "Not when I've got everything ready at last."

With my heart pounding, I snatched them up and ran out through the backyard to the street. But I soon realized how suspicious I must have looked, carrying a bulky flour sack over my shoulder. I couldn't risk meeting up with a policeman or someone I knew, so I doubled back and hid it under some old logs next to our outhouse. I could come back later after dark when it would be safe to carry it away.

35.

When I reached the edge of town, scattered clouds were rushing across the sky in one direction. And, tired of being a burden to my parents, I too was rushing away as fast as I could. One moment the shadow of a cloud passed overhead, making everything dark; then suddenly it would be light again as the shadow moved on, sweeping over distant fields and woods. Other clouds hovered lower, gathering to send rain down on this town where everyone's life is filled with misery, this town where women are sold night and day. I turned to stick out my tongue at Koza but was struck by a sudden gust of wind that drove me up the hill overlooking Misato village. Here the wind hit me head-on, billowing up inside my collar and under my shorts. It felt as if my whole body were being tickled viciously until I was afraid I would be lifted off my feet and hurled up into the sky.

The ocean, seething with white wave crests, was veiled in a thick fog, and the hills on the peninsula beyond were wrapped in a swirling mist of salt spray that hid them almost completely.

As soon as I reached the shore, I ran out to check the wharf. A car was parked in front of the guard shack, and out on the pier a husky American hurried from one side to the other, tightening the ropes that bound the yachts and motor boats to their moorings. Most of the boats had already been covered and tied securely with several bands of thick rope.

I still had to go back for the flour sack, so I shoved my school satchel under a *sabani* boat that lay upside down on the beach.

36.

I ran all the way back to town through a driving rainstorm, but as I passed the store on our block, I saw something that made me stop in my tracks. Four houses down the street, Dad stood in our yard, nailing boards over the front door. He was still wearing his sweaty army fatigue cap, so he must have started preparing for the typhoon as soon as he got home from his job on the base. I also noticed he was using lumber he had taken from the woodpile beside the outhouse, and this meant he would have seen the flour sack I had hidden there. Concealing myself on one side of the store, I watched Dad pounding nails into our front door. I felt as though he were purposely shutting me out of the house, and it made me resent him all the more. Above me, the storekeeper had climbed up onto his roof and was tossing down hunks of firewood. A few feet over his head the power lines made a high screeching sound as they trembled in the wind. Now I had no reason to go back to the house, and no time to waste on regrets.

37.

Leaving town again, I had to struggle against the rising wind as if I were walking through deep water. No matter how much I wriggled and squirmed, I couldn't get my body pointed in the right direction. And the swirling air that filled my mouth and nostrils made it hard even to breathe. The dazzling white beach and lush green island of my dreams awaited me, but try as I might, I could not seem to move forward. Finally, in frustration, I lunged out angrily at the wind, and to my surprise, it yielded. I found that by striking out shoulder first with the full weight of my body, I could thrust myself ahead one step at a time.

The wind swept up sand from the road that stung the skin on my face, arms, and legs; and I could hear the dry, crackling sound of sand smashing against the wooden walls of fishermen's houses. In one yard a man was braving the storm to do some last-minute pruning of the leaves on his banana plants. A sheet of tin roofing torn loose by the wind flew along the road, rattling noisily. I could see it would be dangerous to stay in the village, so I made several quick lunges through the wind and got out of there.

Under a darkening sky, the branches of seaside pines were shrieking in the wind. And I hollered back, on my way at last to the green island of my dreams. Struggling out to one of the pines, I clutched hold of the trunk and looked up at its branches that shook wildly, like the hair of an insane woman. I tried hard to put my arms around her, but, like all women, she was too big for me. From here I could see the guard shack. The windows on three sides were covered with shutters, but the glass door in front was lit up by a lamp inside. I waited under the pine tree, watching the door to see if the silhouette of the guard would appear. The peninsula, the water, and the wharf were now pitch dark; only a patch of ocean spray in front of the glass door shone dimly white in the lamplight. I hoped the guard would say the yacht had broken loose and floated away. That way he couldn't be blamed. And I would be sure to cut the ropes to make it look like an accident.

38.

I crawled low past the guard shack and made my way down to the wharf. I had forgotten to fill the canteen in my school satchel, but it was too late to turn back now.

Out on the pier it was still impossible to stand. Each time I tried to raise myself, the wind sent me sprawling and very nearly knocked me into the boiling ocean below. Though I wanted to make a dash for the boats, I finally had to drop down on all fours and creep forward as though climbing a ladder.

The yachts were tied down more securely than I'd expected. I grabbed the rope and yanked with all my might, but couldn't haul them in any closer to the pier. Each boat was tied in two places, from its stern to the buoy moorings and from its bow to the pier. But only about ten yards separated the boats from the pier, so I decided to scale across. I clutched the ropes of one boat with my arms and legs and, hanging over the water, pulled myself along hand over hand.

The tide rose up thundering around the boats, then crashed down over them. With the surging waves splashing my back violently, I was afraid the rope would sag too low under my weight. Just as I thought I would be swept away, the tide fell back, and half in a daze, I hauled myself along the last stretch of rope and lowered one foot onto a tire that hung from the yacht's gunwale.

Pulling out my knife, I sliced through the canvas boat cover and crawled underneath it. Someone had been careful to lock the cabin door, but nothing could stop me now. The boat cover hid me from view, and no one would be able to hear the noise of my smashing the lock.

The air inside the cabin was thick with the smell of varnish and rope. I squatted dripping wet over a pile of rope and paused to celebrate. "I made it! Aboard at last! Blow, wind, blow! The harder the better!"

The storm was still roaring in toward the shore, but I knew that once the eye of the typhoon passed, the wind would reverse direction. Then I would cut the ropes binding the yacht to its moorings and let the wind carry it out through the bay to the open sea. The stronger the wind, the faster I could get away, and when I reached open water, I would put up the sail.

I crouched down, tightly grasping my knife, and listened to the tide crashing against the hull. As each wave rocked the boat higher and higher, I knew I would soon be carried out to the open sea. Rising through my feet, a surge of violent excitement set my whole body quivering.

Afterword

A child in ecstasy embarks on the voyage of his dreams; a father in despair begins a difficult quest for justice. *Child of Okinawa* and *Cocktail Party* conclude at opposite ends of the emotional spectrum, yet they follow a strikingly similar progression of events. Each protagonist finds himself in circumstances that grow more and more intolerable until he finally sets out on a hazardous course that cuts him off from those around him. And each situation results because the occupation and vast military presence in Okinawa magnify human failings on both sides of the bifurcated society. The father seeks to confront the hypocrisy of occupation law by prosecuting Robert Harris, a decision that separates him from people who had urged, for both altruistic and selfish reasons, that he drop the charges. The boy seeks to escape the degradation of his base town environment, leaving behind all his family and friends.

In literary terms, both stories could be said to contain elements of fictional quest, with idealistic protagonists posed against quasi villains in corrupt and oppressive surroundings.[1] The quests themselves also pass through similar stages. First, each story begins on the edge of the bifurcation with a clear sense that something is wrong. The father feels acutely out of place as he enters the base and becomes increasingly conscious of the deep divisions among the people at the cocktail party, which are only partially camouflaged by its artificial joviality. Tsuneyoshi is already aware of the corruption in his household in the opening scene when he reluctantly lends his bed to Michikō and her GI customer. Second, each protagonist experiences a dramatic awakening that reveals

---

[1] Fictional quest as a literary genre is described by Northrop Frye in *Anatomy of Criticism: Four Essays* (Princeton, N.J.: Princeton University Press, 1957), pp. 186–195.

the wider implications of what is wrong. In *Cocktail Party* the rape makes brutally plain the inequities of occupation rule and shows the devastating effect it can have on personal relationships. From what he sees in Koza, Tsuneyoshi soon learns that the corruption extends far beyond his home to confront him at nearly every turn. And, third, each protagonist wavers and hesitates before embarking on his final course.

Both quests progress within a common narrative structure described by A. T. Greimas as movement away from integration toward alienation, culminating in the breaking of an implicit contract with society.[2] As for *Cocktail Party*, the contract states that in Okinawa a bureaucrat and family man in his forties go along with the system and take what material benefits he can from it, while protecting his private life. The decision to prosecute Harris alienates him from others and threatens the privacy of his family. A child in Okinawa is also expected to go along with things as they are, to cooperate in (or at least not to impede) the family business, to attend school despite troubles with teachers and classmates, and to remain at home even with an abusive father. By stealing a yacht to escape his life in Koza, Tsuneyoshi moves beyond adolescent rebellion to a complete rejection of his society.

Ōshiro and Higashi tell their stories in ways that forcefully draw the reader into each situation and create dramatic settings for the final breaking of these implicit contracts. The two authors relate the experiences of their protagonists with an intensity that is often lacking in protest literature, which depends more for its impact on ringing slogans or revelations of ideological truth. They achieve their most powerful effects by focusing on objects, especially details in particular scenes, that heighten dramatic tension and resonate thematically. Conversely, the impact of the narrative is diminished when statements of theme are placed directly in the mouths of their characters.[3] That these objects are often drawn from nature reflects a prevailing technique of Japanese

---

[2] A. T. Greimas, *Du sens* (Paris: Seuil, 1970), pp. 27–49. Greimas's theory of narrative structure is discussed in Jonathan Culler, *Structuralist Poetics: Structuralism, Linguistics, and the Study of Literature* (Ithaca, N.Y.: Cornell University Press, 1975), p. 214. I have used Culler's English translations of Greimas's terminology.

[3] Roland Barthes writes of the evocative power of "objects" as opposed to "concepts" in *Essais critiques* (Paris: Seuil, 1964), p. 32. Portions are translated and discussed in Culler, p. 194. Masao Miyoshi notes Japanese novelists' preference for "suggestion and evocation" in *Accomplices of Silence: The Modern Japanese Novel* (Berkeley and Los Angeles: University of California Press, 1974), p. xv.

literature, ancient and modern, which is applied with ingenuity to the special environment of Okinawa. Higashi's evocations of local flora and fauna are often startling, even bizarre, while Ōshiro uses natural phenomena for effects that are usually more subdued. The oppressive heat and humidity at the opening of *Cocktail Party* help convey the protagonist's uneasiness as he enters the base. The sharp bifurcation between Okinawa's military and civilian worlds is apparent in the contrast between the expanse of symmetrical lawns inside the family brigade and the lush, rugged landscape outside the American enclave. Perhaps the natural objects that resonate longest in the reader's mind come appropriately at the end of this story. As the protagonist walks over the very ground on beautiful Cape M. where his daughter was attacked, he finds it "incredible that this peaceful landscape" with its soft breezes and gently splashing waves "had been the scene of a crime." The image works both to communicate by implied contrast the turmoil inside him and to show how indifferent nature can be in the face of tumultuous human events. The reader never learns the outcome of his daughter's trial, but such ironic posing of natural imagery, typical of classical Japanese poetry,[4] frames the preceding narrative and gives the story a sense of closure.[5]

Like Ōshiro, Higashi focuses on natural objects to convey emotion and enhance dramatic impact, but he uses them thematically in ways that Ōshiro does not. Nature provides a refuge for Tsuneyoshi's escapes from home and school. He flees to quiet valleys, grassy hillsides, and deserted beaches after run-ins with his parents, classmates, and teacher. He even seeks the ultimate escape to nature in his planned voyage to an uninhabited island, inspired partly by his reading *The Adventures of Robinson Crusoe*. These benevolent manifestations of the natural environment are balanced by references to its threatening aspects—snakes, insects,

---

[4] Exemplified by this well-known travel verse composed by Matsuo Bashō (1644–1694) on his visit to the site of an ancient fortress.

Natsugusa ya	Summer grass—
Tsuwamono-domo ga	All that remains
Yume no ato	Of soldiers' dreams.

[5] Victor Shklovsky calls such conclusions "illusory endings" in "La construction de la nouvelle et du roman," in Tzvetan Todorov, ed., *Theorie de la litterature* (Paris: Seuil, 1965), pp. 176–177. Portions translated in Culler, p. 223. "Usually it is descriptions of nature or of weather that furnish material for these illusory endings....This new motif is inscribed as a parallel to the preceding story, thanks to which the tale seems completed."

sharks, swirling ocean tides, and a typhoon (also used to fore-shadow the crisis in *Cocktail Party*) that heighten moments of tension in the narrative.

In a later story, Higashi chooses many of the same objects Ōshiro evokes to highlight the incongruity of America's vast military presence in Okinawa and the sharp economic divisions it perpetuates. The narrator of *Churakāgi* (Good-lookin', 1976) describes base housing from his childhood memories in a passage strongly reminiscent of the opening of *Cocktail Party*.

> The place was a wide expanse of gently rolling hills with valleys and small groves of trees. Paved streets wound out in all directions, and houses with red-tiled roofs and white siding dotted the landscape. This was the housing area where American families lived. Everywhere I looked were grassy lawns and flower gardens. In one yard children played, their golden hair fluttering in the breeze, while a young housewife looked out at them from her garden of flowering trees. Her brown hair was tied up with a ribbon, and her arms and legs gleamed white. Bicycles lay by the side of the road where children had left them and toys were strewn on the lawns. Though we were just passing through, the place seemed like a different world that made our hearts beat faster.[6]

In *Child of Okinawa*, however, Higashi's natural imagery differs markedly from Ōshiro's in the startling way it accentuates more disturbing manifestations of the military presence. Fleeing the sounds of a prostitute plying her trade in his room, Tsuneyoshi sees that the sky over Koza is lit by "the pale glow of neon." Moments later he lies in a quiet valley, relieved to be looking up at a sky where "only the stars shone." A similar juxtaposition sets the "glaring patrol lights" of an American battleship in the bay against the serenity of a purple sky at dawn. In more disquieting similes, Tsuneyoshi likens small naval craft rusting on a beach shortly after the war to flies surrounding a corpse and compares the growth of Koza along the base highway to "ants swarming around a worm." The countless used condoms he discovers floating in Koza's overflowing sewage remind him of "maggots... coil[ing] with lust." It is a spectacle that both disgusts and arouses him.

Besides natural phenomena, other visual details move these stories dramatically and thematically. Nowhere is the corruption

---

[6] *Churakāgi* (Good-lookin'), in Higashi Mineo, *Okinawa no shōnen* (Bungei Shunjū, 1980), p. 233.

of Koza more powerfully conveyed than when Tsuneyoshi's mother tells Michikō that heated water for her douche can be found beside the family altar, or moments later when she reaches down in desperation to gather up the remnants of dollar bills paid to Michikō that Tsuneyoshi has ripped to bits in a burst of adolescent righteousness. And perhaps the object that resonates longest in this story is the little dry spot Tsuneyoshi finds early one foggy morning under a pair of woman's panties left on a wet Koza street. In *Cocktail Party* Ōshiro reveals the superficiality of the characters' "international friendship" by focusing on gestures, facial expressions, and other unspoken signals that often carry messages inconsistent with what the people in the story are saying. Through such clues he shows the deep disagreements and misunderstandings that hover just below the surface of the cocktail party chatter. Virtually every dispute that threatens to upset party decorum is averted by nonverbal means. In awkward moments the guests turn to the generous outlays of food and liquor to avoid conflict. Mr. Ogawa excuses himself for a refill of his drink to escape the persistent Mr. Morgan. To stem further discussions with Morgan, the protagonist takes a large bite of food; later he lifts his glass to his mouth rather than join the argument between Mr. Ogawa and Mr. Sun about Japanese pirates. Mr. Miller hides his "obvious discomfort" over the mention of a Chinese Communist writer by "taking a furtive sip of his drink."

The rape that begins the second half of the story brings the conflict to the surface. Seeking to confront his daughter's assailant, the protagonist asks for help from people whose perceptions of self-interest quickly outweigh their concern for international friendship. Again, gestures, silences, and facial expressions often reveal far more than words. When the protagonist pleads with Mr. Miller to accompany him to the hospital, Miller replies coldly that anyone can enter there if they "follow the proper procedures." Although he does not say so, Miller's response, an indirect refusal, makes it clear that he has already decided to avoid involvement in the protagonist's situation. In the next scene, at Mr. Ogawa's apartment, the protagonist recalls, "When I asked [Mr. Miller] for help, he suddenly turned cold and businesslike."

Unspoken signals propel the narrative of *Cocktail Party* to a remarkable degree, considering the many provocative discussions among its characters. It is on occasions when the dialogue becomes overburdened with statements of theme that the impact momentarily diminishes. Near the end, for example, the protagonist rather too neatly (and unnecessarily) sums things up when he announces his intention to "indict" the cocktail party as well as Robert Harris. The extended dialogue in this scene, while probing crucial issues of justice and reconciliation, deflates the drama of the final confrontation and makes his outraged exit from the club less than climactic.

In *Child of Okinawa* Tsuneyoshi also appears to make thematic statements when he tells his mother to "quit selling women" and condemns Koza as "this town where women are sold night and day." But rather than suggesting the polemic intrusion of the author, Tsuneyoshi's comments fit into the narrative because they sound typical of adolescents everywhere who denounce the compromises their elders view as practical necessities for getting along in the world. Tsuneyoshi's outrage is not so different from that of Holden Caulfield in *The Catcher in the Rye*, who condemns "phoniness" in wealthy suburbia where status, rather than survival, is everyone's obsession.[7] Despite the sordid circumstances of Tsuneyoshi's life in Koza, his story is told with buoyancy. In contrast, the rape intensifies a mood of darkness and foreboding that settles over *Cocktail Party* after some humorous moments during the party itself. Critic Kitazawa Miho writes of a "paradoxical brightness" that emanates because *Child of Okinawa* is actually "the Okinawa of a child," a story told through the eyes of an adolescent boy with a lively imagination.[8] The viewpoint that creates this tone is reflected in both language and form. While Ōshiro's dialogue and narration are cast in the more refined idiom of highly educated and widely traveled adults, *Child of Okinawa* is narrated almost entirely as a young adolescent speaking. Like J. D. Salinger, Higashi has adroitly captured the lilt and naive directness in the speech of a boy in his early teens.[9] The author wavers from this idiom on a few occasions for brief poetic renderings of such natural phenomena as pine needles rustling in the breeze or the ocean at sunset, but transitions back and forth are so smooth that the reader hardly notices the change.

---

[7] J. D. Salinger, *The Catcher in the Rye* (New York: Little, Brown, 1945).

[8] Kitazawa Miho, "Kaisetsu" (Commentary), in Higashi, *Okinawa no shōnen* (1980), p. 276.

[9] Narrative voice is established in the opening phrase "Boku ga nete iru to ne" ("I was asleep when … ").

When characters speak with one another, Higashi infuses almost everyone's conversation with Okinawa dialect.[10] He does this mostly by using words that vary in obvious ways from standard Japanese (actually Tokyo dialect) since most readers on the mainland would not be able to understand dialogue that differed widely from standard speech. Thus, the standard *okosu* (to awaken someone) becomes *ukosu; okire* (the imperative "wake up") becomes *ukire; tago* (a wooden bucket) becomes *tagō;* and the name Michiko becomes Michikō. Okinawa dialect, like standard Japanese, contains distinct levels of politeness and formality manifested in the structure of nouns and verbs. The rough, bantering exchanges in this story, so different from the mostly polite conversation in *Cocktail Party,* are punctuated with dialectical interjections and pungent barbs. Tsuneyoshi's mother expresses her homespun survival philosophy in especially blunt language when she scolds him.

As noted above, the stories also differ markedly in form, although both are essentially first-person narratives. Throughout *Child of Okinawa* the pronoun of narration is the informal *boku* (I) typical of boys and young men. The switch in the middle of *Cocktail Party* from the formal *watakushi* (I) to the informal *omae* (you) creates a tone of self-criticism throughout the second half of the story. At this point the narrator-protagonist, who now seems to be addressing himself, tells how he discovered, through the crisis precipitated by the rape, that he had been "fooled" by the party's illusion of international friendship.

The thirty-eight short chapters in *Child of Okinawa* include both episodes in chronological order and flashbacks to Tsuneyoshi's earlier childhood. Their loose, disjointed sequence enhances the impression of a young adolescent telling his story with digressions of opinion and emotion that an adult would be less likely to make. Although Ōshiro's two-part format is also subdivided into episodes, present happenings and past memories are woven more smoothly into the narrative. Both works contain considerable interior monologue, but the dark, self-doubting ruminations in *Cocktail Party* contrast sharply with Tsuneyoshi's wide-ranging fantasies and ambitious daydreams. Ōshiro's protagonist ponders the connection between wartime atrocities and the attack on his daughter until he feels compelled to act in pursuit of justice. Tsuneyoshi

---

[10] The exception is Tsuneyoshi's teacher, Miss Asato, who speaks in standard Japanese, the language of the classroom in public schools.

relives pleasant childhood memories and imagines the future, as
children often do when caught in troubled circumstances, until he
is finally driven to "act out" his most cherished fantasy.

Tsuneyoshi's troubles have much to do with the circumstances
of his sexual awakening, but the situations he finds himself in are
often charged with humor. When asked to relinquish his bed so
two GI customers can be accommodated simultaneously, he sug-
gests that both couples use one bed together. He questions the
soldiers' need to buy sex from women after his discovery of mas-
turbation. And those who patronize Koza, far from being lust-
crazed warriors, often seem little more than children themselves,
unable to hold their liquor or control their bladders and, on one
occasion, too nervous to engage in the sex they have paid for.
Tsuneyoshi's bittersweet meeting with Chiiko in his room, where
she comes closest to teaching him "the facts of life," is perhaps the
most finely crafted episode in the story for the way certain details
(his flute-playing, "her red-painted lips," and the sounds of
another night's business in Koza) convey his ambiguous feelings
toward sex. As for the women who work in the bars, they live, by
day at least, almost as members of Tsuneyoshi's family (he compares Chiiko to "a big sister"), sharing meals, household chores,
leisurely trips to the public bath, and long gossip sessions in
which they exchange humorous anecdotes about past customers.
Tsuneyoshi's mother displays a kind of motherly concern for
them, too. They even make a show of affection toward the soldiers who purchase their services, though the dangers of their
work are vividly exemplified in the grenade thrown at Chiiko's
bar by a disappointed admirer.

This brief glimpse of violence and the story's conclusion have
puzzled some readers. Chiiko appears to have been Tsuneyoshi's
first love, yet he makes no response when overhearing another bar
girl tell how the explosion left "burns all over her face." Could his
determination to leave Koza or his discoveries about Chiiko have
removed him emotionally from her to this extent? The author
does not say. An unexplained turnabout also occurs in *Cocktail
Party* when, at the end of the story, the daughter has agreed to
cooperate in the prosecution of her assailant after steadfastly
opposing it all along. Her father's earlier observation that, since
the rape, she seems to have drifted away from the influence of her
parents makes her apparent change of heart all the more mystify-
ing. In reviewing this story, novelist and critic Ishikawa Tatsuzō

said he would have preferred a fuller rendering of her feelings.[11]

Perhaps speculating on characters' motives is part of the experience of reading. And the same might be said of interpreting fictional endings that raise questions about what has happened in a story up to that point. Still, while *Child of Okinawa* has been widely praised, some in Japan criticized the ambiguities surrounding Tsuneyoshi's final escape, calling this conclusion "tacked on" and "contrived for effect."[12]

In several respects the end seems to follow logically from Tsuneyoshi's growing defiance of his parents, his increasing absences from home and school, and his intense preparations for his voyage. There are, of course, serious doubts about his prospects for survival (lack of essential supplies or sailing experience). And the reader wonders in retrospect about the significance of ominous hints dropped earlier regarding Tsuneyoshi's future (black birds, a strangely frightening sunset, and the ghost of a recent drowning victim). These highly foreboding signs also raise a fundamental question about the time and place from which Tsuneyoshi narrates the story. Could its many references to death, especially to tombs and cemeteries, which are important religious artifacts in Okinawa, suggest that he is telling it from beyond the grave? Again, the author gives no answers. Yet, for this reader, such mysteries only enhance the evocative power of what is, after all, a work of fiction.

Comments on ambiguities of characterization and plot came amidst critical acclaim in Japan for both authors' treatment of highly charged contemporary issues through the medium of fiction.[13] Less illuminating were attempts in the popular press to categorize these stories with the labels "anti-American" and "antiwar." To be sure, Mr. Miller does seem to play the villain in *Cocktail Party*, especially when he is viewed within Northrup

---

[11] The comments of Ishikawa and other members of the Akutagawa Prize Selection Committee precede the story in *Bungei shunjū* 65:9 (September 1967): 317.

[12] See comments of Akutagawa Selection Committee members Nakamura Mitsuo and Funahashi Seiichi which precede the story in *Bungei shunjū* 50:3 (March 1972): 315 and 317. Funahashi speculates that Tsuneyoshi's escape has an autobiographical parallel in Higashi's departure from Okinawa to live on the mainland in 1964.

[13] As a member of the Akutagawa Selection Committee, Nobel Prize–winning novelist Kawabata Yasunari commented that *Cocktail Party* "succeeds in making us feel that the problems depicted extend far beyond Okinawa" (*Bungei shunjū* 65:9 [September 1967]: 322). Of *Child of Okinawa* Kitazawa Miho wrote, "The drama is universal, transcending time and place to reveal the inner workings of the human spirit (see "Kaisetsu," in Higashi, *Okinawa no shōnen* [1980], p. 277).

Frye's broad definition of a fictional quest. "Characters tend to be either for or against the quest," Frye writes, and those who "obstruct it" are portrayed as "villainous or cowardly."[14] Although Mr. Miller's obstruction takes a passive form, the hypocrisy of his pompous pronouncements about international friendship is fully revealed in his attitude toward a friend in trouble. He is determined to exploit the others for Chinese language practice (refusing even to speak English with them) and callously ignores the protagonist's feelings. Robert Harris might also be seen as a villain, but with his limited characterization he seems cast more in the role of a catalyst.

Yet Americans are not the only ones depicted unfavorably. Even Mr. Sun, portrayed sympathetically throughout most of the story, gives his help very grudgingly. And Mr. Ogawa, who accuses Mr. Sun of cowardice, reveals the limits of his own courage when he fails ignominiously to support the protagonist at moments of confrontation and abruptly reverses his stand on prosecution near the end. Besides, had the author wanted to single out one country for condemnation, it seems unlikely that he would have made atrocities committed by Japanese and Chinese soldiers crucial elements in the story. And, finally, with the protagonist stating "I understand why the present international situation requires American bases in Okinawa," even his explicit criticism of U.S. foreign policy is restricted to occupation rule, though the bases are described throughout the story with a tone of deep apprehension.

Higashi depicts the negative effects of the American military presence more extensively in *Child of Okinawa*. Aside from Koza's "amusement area," there are references to land seizures (the runway in Grandfather's field and the refugees from Isahama) as well as GI crime (Kōkichi's accident and the attack on Chiiko's bar). Yet American soldiers are hardly villains in this story, that honor being reserved for Tsuneyoshi's father. In fact, Tsuneyoshi's indignation is aimed far more at his parents for running "this lousy business" than at those who patronize it. Furthermore, it seems unlikely that a story intended to malign the United States would include the U.S.-funded Ryūkyū-American Friendship Center where Tsuneyoshi bones up for his voyage or the goat he remembers fondly that his family received under a commodities aid program through the U.S. Department of Agriculture. Rather,

---

14 Frye, p. 195.

Child of Okinawa seems to reflect the ambivalent feelings of many in Okinawa toward the United States.

Reading either of these stories as antiwar literature raises similar problems. The narrator of *Cocktail Party* describes the horrors of war at several points, but rather than condemning war itself, he focuses on the responsibility of individuals for their actions at the battlefront and in areas under military occupation. Moreover, his statement that he understands the need for American bases in Okinawa would seem to preclude a pacifist interpretation of this work. Tsuneyoshi is troubled by his memories of World War II in Saipan and expresses a strong aversion to such instruments of war as battleships, landing craft, and rifles, although he tries unsuccessfully near the end of the story to locate a gun for his voyage. Still, if showing the negative effects of an enormous military presence can be equated with opposing war, there might be some justification for applying the antiwar label to *Child of Okinawa.* Somehow this seems to be stretching a point.

Readers might have been tempted to pin such labels on these stories because of the considerable amount of literature from Okinawa, especially poetry, with far more explicit political and philosophical messages. These writings have dealt with the 1945 battle as well as the U.S. occupation and military presence. Yamanokuchi Baku, perhaps the best-known modern poet from Okinawa, wrote "Okinawa yo doko e iku" (Whither Okinawa) just before the signing of the 1951 peace treaty that, in his words, "severed Okinawa from the rest of Japan."[15] Strongly atypical of Yamanokuchi's work in its didactic character, this poem gives a historical summary in verse of Okinawa's past connections with Japan and China, concluding with this final exhortation:

> Japan—the nation that wreaked on you
> war's foolish havoc.
> And yet,
> oh Okinawa,
> though your wounds are deep,
> you must recover and return.[16]

---

[15] "Yamanokuchi Baku," in *Nihon no shika* (Poetry of Japan) (Chūo Kōron Sha, 1969), p. 366.

[16] Yamanokuchi Baku, "Okinawa yo doko e iku," in Yamanokuchi Baku, *Maguro ni iwashi* (Tuna and sardines) (Hara Shobō, 1964), pp. 152–159.

In his 1972 poem "Okinawa," Shiro Yū (b. 1932) draws a connection between the ordeal of local residents, who crowded into caves attempting to survive the 1945 battle, and the problems people faced during the U.S. involvement in Vietnam, when the island was used as a training ground and staging area for U.S. forces deployed to Southeast Asia.

> After all these years
> we are still in a cave
> that has no exit.
> . . . .
>
> I remember my sister,
> screaming in terror as she tried to stay alive.
> Her bones have long been buried here,
> but still we cannot leave.
> Out in the countryside
> where we should hear waves breaking on the rocks
> and turtledoves calling from trees grown thick,
> our eardrums are assaulted
> with the clatter of tanks and bulldozers
> crawling over the earth,
> with the roar of jets climbing and diving,
> then napalm shells bursting.
> (Yes, war goes on as before.)
>
> And, much like twenty-six years ago,
> we huddle together
> in this cave with no exit,
> our heads lowered,
> our arms embracing,
> face to face,
> . . . .
> no longer able to cry.[17]

Shiro's more recent "Soshite sengo" (And then came "postwar", 1982) voices protest themes common in Okinawa since reversion— the island's continuing militarization and the apparent insensitivity of many who visit from the mainland.

> Ten years after the reversion pact
> Okinawa has changed, they say.

---

[17] Shiro Yū, "Okinawa," in Tsuboi Shigeji, ed., *Nihon no teikō-shi* (Japan's poetry of protest) (Kōwa-dō, 1974), pp. 300–302.

In Naha new buildings
and hotels that line the street
tower over people walking by;
and now highways circling the island
are nicely paved, they say.

． ． ． ． ． ． ． ． ． ． ． ． ． ．

Thousands from the mainland
come each year
to buy postcards, drink the local rice liquor,
and gaze at traditional fabrics and dyes.
They gather sea shells
while sipping Coca-Cola
and toss away the empty cans.

Happy honeymooners,
arriving at the beach,
pull off their clothes.
Then, after breathless embraces,
they board buses to tour the battle sites
and take turns posing for snapshots
in front of Shirayuri Shrine,
laughing all the while.

Yes, Okinawa has surely changed
these past ten years.
A generation that never saw the war
and knows it only from words printed and spoken
has swelled in numbers
while those who lived through it
are decreasing day by day.

But on the U.S. air base at Kadena
F-4s and F-15s still stand ready day and night
to fly off and make war
anywhere on earth.
And from their bases at Ginowan
the latest weapons of mass murder
reach up with muzzles poised, awaiting orders.

What has changed with the reversion pact
is that now Japan's Self-Defense Forces
proudly guard America's bases
with P-2J sub-spotter planes they fly around the clock,
keeping watch over the vast Pacific's waves.
Because in all these "postwar" years
one thing has never changed:
The Pentagon still runs this island.[18]

---

[18] Shiro Yū, "Soshite sengo," in *Shijin kaigi* (Poets' conference) 20:5 (May 1982): 26–27.

Considering the prevalence of such writings and the tenor of the times when *Cocktail Party* and *Child of Okinawa* first appeared, the temptation to read too much ideology into these stories was perhaps understandable. They are deeply affecting portrayals of what it is like to live under prolonged foreign occupation amidst a vast military presence. What finally makes it hard to categorize them is their focus on the experience of each individual protagonist in a way that reveals how circumstances in Okinawa exacerbate more widespread human conflicts—the strains of adolescence, the pressures of poverty, and the vulnerability of friendship under stress. They are compelling because they represent a particular, and to most of us unfamiliar, situation within the context of difficulties faced by people everywhere.

About the Authors

Ōshiro Tatsuhiro was born September 19, 1925, in Nakagusuku, Okinawa Prefecture. After completing middle school, he attended a prestigious academy in Shanghai, returning to Okinawa at the end of World War II. During the U.S. occupation he taught high school, worked in the Trade Office of the Government of the Ryukyu Islands, and later served as director of the Okinawa Institute of Historical Collections. Beginning his writing career shortly after the war, he has published numerous books and articles on Okinawa's culture and history as well as works of fiction and drama (see bibliography). *Cocktail Party* first appeared in the magazine *Shin Okinawa bungaku* (New literature of Okinawa) in February 1967. Awarded an Akutagawa Prize in September, it was included as the title work in a collection of his stories published the same year by Bungei Shunjū press and has been reissued in two subsequent collections. His fiction has been acclaimed for skillfully rendering Okinawan cultural motifs and for portraying tumultuous events during and after World War II from the historical and psychological perspective of people in Okinawa.

Higashi Mineo was born May 15, 1938, in Mindanao, The Philippines. Returning with his family to Okinawa after World War II, he attended high school in Koza City and worked for the U.S. military on nearby Kadena Air Base. In 1964 he moved to Tokyo, where he took temporary jobs to support himself while concentrating on his writing. *Child of Okinawa* first appeared in *Bungakkai* (Literary world) magazine in December 1971. Awarded an Akutagawa Prize the next year, it was published by Bungei Shunjū press as the title work for a hardback volume of his fiction in 1972 and for a paperback collection in 1980. Chūō Kōron press published *Ōki na hato no kage* (Shadow of a big dove), a collection of eleven new stories, in 1981. Two years later a Japanese film entitled (in

English) *Okinawan Boys,* directed by Shinjō Taku, was released; it draws loosely on characters and episodes from *Child of Okinawa.* Higashi's fiction, which often depicts the encounters of people from Okinawa with Americans and mainland Japanese, has been praised widely for its stylistic innovation and its lyricism.

Steve Rabson is Associate Professor in the Department of East Asian Studies at Brown University. He received a Ph.D. from Harvard University in 1979. His publications include articles on the fiction of Ōe Kenzaburō and Nagai Kafū and the poetry of Kaneko Mitsuharu and Yamanokuchi Baku. His book *Righteous Cause or Tragic Folly: Changing Views of War in Modern Japanese Poetry* is forthcoming from the University of Michigan Center for Japanese Studies.

Bibliography

Arasaki Moriteru. *Sengo Okinawa-shi* (Postwar Okinawan history). Nihon Hyōron Sha, 1982.

Arazato Kinbuku and Ōshiro Tatsuhiro. *Kindai Okinawa no ayumi* (The course of modern Okinawan history). Taihei Shuppansha, 1972.

———. *Kindai Okinawa no hitobito* (A who's who of modern Okinawa). Taihei Shuppansha, 1972.

Asahi Shinbun Sha, ed. *Okinawa hōkoku* (Reports from Okinawa). Asahi Shinbun Sha, 1969.

Ahagon Chōshō. *Okinawa bunka-shi* (A cultural history of Okinawa). Naha: Okinawa Taimusu Sha, 1970.

Barthes, Roland. *Essais critiques.* Paris: Seuil, 1964.

Central Intelligence Agency. "The Ryukyu Islands and Their Significance." Report of August 6, 1948. Washington, D.C.: Government Printing Office, 1948.

Culler, Jonathan. *Structuralist Poetics: Structuralism, Linguistics, and the Study of Literature.* Ithaca, N.Y.: Cornell University Press, 1975.

Fisch, Arnold G., Jr. *Military Government in the Ryukyu Islands 1945–1950.* Washington, D.C.: Center of Military History, United States Army, 1988.

Frye, Northrup. *Anatomy of Criticism: Four Essays.* Princeton, N.J.: Princeton University Press, 1957.

Funahashi Seiichi. "Jushō-saku nihen" (The two prizewinning works). *Bungei shunjū* 50:3 (March 1972): 317.

Gibe Keishun, Aniya Masaaki, and Kurima Yasuo. *Sengo Okinawa no rekishi* (Postwar history of Okinawa). Nihon Seinen Shuppansha, 1971.

Greimas, A. J. *Du sens.* Paris: Seuil, 1970.

Havens, Thomas R. H. *Fire across the Sea: The Vietnam War and Japan, 1965–1975.* Princeton, N.J.: Princeton University Press, 1987.

Higa Mikio. *Politics and Parties in Postwar Okinawa.* Vancouver: University of British Columbia Press, 1963.

Higashi Mineo. *Okinawa no shōnen* (Child of Okinawa). Bungei Shunjū, 1972.

———. *Okinawa no shōnen* (Child of Okinawa). Bungei Shunjū, 1980. This paperback collection includes commentary by Kitazawa Miho.

_____. *Ōki na hato no kage* (Shadow of a big dove). Chūō Kōron Sha, 1981.

Higashimatsu Teruaki. *Okinawa ni kichi ga aru* (Bases in Okinawa). Gurabia Seikō Sha, 1969.

Hokama Shuzen. *Okinawa bungaku no sekai* (The world of Okinawan literature). Kadokawa Shoten, 1979.

Ienaga, Saburō. *The Pacific War.* Translated by Frank Baldwin. New York: Pantheon, 1978. Original is *Taiheiyō sensō.* Iwanami Shoten, 1968.

Ishikawa Tatsuzō. "Tōsen o iwau" (A tribute to the prizewinning entries). *Bungei shunjū* 45:9 (September 1967): 317.

Joint Chiefs of Staff. "Draft Directive to Commander-in-Chief, Far East for Military Government of the Ryukyu Islands, July 29, 1949." Reprinted in *Foreign Relations* 7 (1949): 816–819.

Kano Masanao. *Sengo Okinawa no shisō zō* (Trends of thought in postwar Okinawa). Asahi Shinbun Sha, 1987.

Kawabata Yasunari. "Tekisetsu na settei" (A well-chosen setting). *Bungei shunjū* 45:9 (September 1967): 322.

Kennan, George F. "Conversation between General of the Army MacArthur and Mr. George F. Kennan, March 5, 1948." *Foreign Relations* 6 (1948): 699–706.

Kerr, George. *Okinawa: The History of an Island People.* Rutland, Vt.: Tuttle, 1958.

Kitazawa Miho. "Kaisetsu" (Commentary). In Higashi Mineo, *Okinawa no shōnen* (Child of Okinawa), pp. 276–281. Bungei Shunjū, 1980.

Makise Tsuneji. *Okinawa no rekishi* (History of Okinawa), vol. 3. Chōbunsha, 1971.

Martin, Jo Nobuko. *A Princess Lily of the Ryukyus.* Tokyo: Shin Nippon Kyōiku Tosho, 1984.

Miyoshi, Masao. *Accomplices of Silence: The Modern Japanese Novel.* Berkeley and Los Angeles: University of California Press, 1974.

Morris, M. D. *Okinawa: A Tiger by the Tail.* New York: Hawthorn, 1968.

Nakamura Mitsuo. "Sainō no tsukaikata ni asobu" (The casual uses of talent). *Bungei shunjū* 50:3 (March 1972): 314–315.

Nihon no shika (Poetry of Japan), vol. 20. Includes selected poems of Yamanokuchi Baku with commentary. Chūō Kōron Sha, 1969.

Ōe Kenzaburō. *Okinawa keiken* (Okinawa experiences). Iwanami Shoten, 1981. Includes collection of essays entitled *Okinawa nōto* (Notes on Okinawa) originally published by Iwanami Shoten in 1970. See Preface.

Ogawa Tōru et al. *Okinawa bunka kenkyū* (Studies in Okinawan culture). Hōsei Daigaku Shuppankyoku, 1975.

Okinawa no kichi (Bases in Okinawa). Naha: Okinawa Taimusu Sha, 1984.

Okinawa Prefectural Government. "Heiwa no ishiji" (Monument of peace). Pamphlet. Naha, Okinawa, 1995.

Ōshiro Tatsuhiro. *Okinawa rekishi sanpo* (A walk through Okinawan history). Sōgensha, 1980.

_____. *Watakushi no Okinawa kyōiku-ron* (My views on education in Okinawa). Essays. Wakanatsusha, 1980.

_____. *Hannyashingyō nyūmon* (An introduction to the Heart Sutra). Essays. Kōbunsha, 1981.

_____. *Kakuteru pātī* (Cocktail Party). Latest edition included with other fiction. Rironsha, 1982.

_____. *Tsushima-maru* (The ship *Tsushima*). Documentary. Rironsha, 1982.

_____. *Asa, Shanhai ni tachitsukusu* (Standing in the Shanghai morning). A novel. Kōdansha, 1983.

_____. *Noro* (Priestess). Fiction. Kōdansha, 1983.

_____. *Hana no ishibumi* (Monument of flowers). Fiction. Kōdansha, 1986.

_____. *Kyūsoku no enerugī—Ajia no naka no Okinawa* (The energy of rest—Okinawa in Asia). Ningen Sensho, 1987. Also see entries under Arazato Kinbuku.

Ōta Masahide. "War Memories Die Hard in Okinawa." *Japan Quarterly* 34:4 (January–March 1988): 9–16.

Reischauer, Edwin O. *The Japanese.* Tokyo: Tuttle, 1977.

_____. *My Life Between Japan and America.* New York: Harper and Row, 1986.

Ryūkyū Shinpō Sha, ed. *Kichi Okinawa* (Okinawa's bases). Simul, 1968.

Salinger, J. D. *The Catcher in the Rye.* New York: Little, Brown, 1945.

Seidensticker, E. G. "The View from Okinawa." *Japan Quarterly* 6:1 (January–March 1959): 37–42.

Seldon, Mark. "Okinawa and American Security Imperialism." In *Remaking Asia: Essays on the American Uses of Power,* ed. Mark Seldon, pp. 279–302. New York: Pantheon, 1974.

Shijin kaigi (Poets' conference). "Okinawa tokushū" (Special issue on Okinawa) 20:5 (May 1982).

Shimabukuro Kazuya. *Fukki-go no Okinawa* (Okinawa after reversion). Kyōikusha, 1979.

Shinzato Keiji, Taminato Tomoaki, and Kinjō Seitoku. *Okinawa-ken no rekishi* (The history of Okinawa prefecture). Yamakawa, 1980.

Shklovsky, Victor. "La construction de la nouvelle et du roman." In *Theorie de la litterature,* ed. Tzvetan Todorov, pp. 170–196. Paris: Seuil, 1965.

Watanabe, Akio. *The Okinawa Problem: A Chapter in Japan-U.S. Relations.* Melbourne, Australia: Melbourne University Press, 1970.

Yamanokuchi Baku. *Maguro ni iwashi* (Tuna and sardines). A collection of his poetry. Hara Shobō, 1964.

INSTITUTE OF EAST ASIAN STUDIES PUBLICATIONS SERIES

CHINA RESEARCH MONOGRAPHS (CRM)

33. Yue Daiyun. *Intellectuals in Chinese Fiction,* 1988
34. Constance Squires Meaney. *Stability and the Industrial Elite in China and the Soviet Union,* 1988
35. Yitzhak Shichor. *East Wind over Arabia: Origins and Implications of the Sino-Saudi Missile Deal,* 1989
36. Suzanne Pepper. *China's Education Reform in the 1980s: Policies, Issues, and Historical Perspectives,* 1990
sp. Phyllis Wang and Donald A. Gibbs, eds. *Readers' Guide to China's Literary Gazette, 1949–1979,* 1990
38. James C. Shih. *Chinese Rural Society in Transition: A Case Study of the Lake Tai Area, 1368–1800,* 1992
39. Anne Gilks. *The Breakdown of the Sino-Vietnamese Alliance, 1970–1979,* 1992
sp. Theodore Han and John Li. *Tiananmen Square Spring 1989: A Chronology of the Chinese Democracy Movement,* 1992
40. Frederic Wakeman, Jr., and Wen-hsin Yeh, eds. *Shanghai Sojourners,* 1992
41. Michael Schoenhals. *Doing Things with Words in Chinese Politics: Five Studies,* 1992
sp. Kaidi Zhan. *The Strategies of Politeness in the Chinese Language,* 1992
42. Barry C. Keenan. *Imperial China's Last Classical Academies: Social Change in the Lower Yangzi, 1864–1911,* 1994
43. Ole Bruun. *Business and Bureaucracy in a Chinese City: An Ethnography of Private Business Households in Contemporary China,* 1993
44. Wei Li. *The Chinese Staff System: A Mechanism for Bureaucratic Control and Integration,* 1994
45. Ye Wa and Joseph W. Esherick. *Chinese Archives: An Introductory Guide,* 1996
46. Melissa Brown, ed. *Negotiating Ethnicities in China and Taiwan,* 1996
47. David Zweig and Chen Changgui. *China's Brain Drain to the United States: Views of Overseas Chinese Students and Scholars in the 1990s,* 1995
48. Elizabeth J. Perry, ed. *Putting Class in Its Place: Worker Identities in East Asia,* 1996

KOREA RESEARCH MONOGRAPHS (KRM)

13. Vipan Chandra. *Imperialism, Resistance, and Reform in Late Nineteenth-Century Korea: Enlightenment and the Independence Club,* 1988
14. Seok Choong Song. *Explorations in Korean Syntax and Semantics,* 1988
15. Robert A. Scalapino and Dalchoong Kim, eds. *Asian Communism: Continuity and Transition,* 1988
16. Chong-Sik Lee and Se-Hee Yoo, eds. *North Korea in Transition,* 1991
17. Nicholas Eberstadt and Judith Banister. *The Population of North Korea,* 1992
18. Hong Yung Lee and Chung Chongwook, eds. *Korean Options in a Changing International Order,* 1993
19. Tae Hwan Ok and Hong Yung Lee, eds. *Prospects for Change in North Korea,* 1994
20. Chai-sik Chung. *A Korean Confucian Encounter with the Modern World: Yi Hang-no and the West,* 1995
21. Myung Hun Kang. *The Korean Business Conglomerate: Chaebol Then and Now,* 1996